CW00394611

CHAPTER 1

4.00am and Alan Da Silva skips off an escalator.

He winks at a giant Jack of Spades and glides into the Crown Casino car park, failing to notice the dark sedan creeping past the adjacent stairwell.

Brushing back his dyed blonde hair, he walks briskly towards his late model Mercedes convertible.

The dark sedan turns to follow him.

Da Silva stops, takes a packet of cigarettes from his pocket and wedges one between his lips. With a deft flick of his silver Zippo he lights up, rocking his head back, as he draws the smoke into his lungs.

He cannot hear the engine of the dark sedan, given the constant hum of the air conditioning system overhead. Nor does he sense how quickly the car has accelerated until it is upon him.

Da Silva turns sharply, blinded by a sudden flash of light. The car's high beam neatly reflected in the thick gold bracelet that dangles from his wrist, as he tries to shield his eyes.

A mesh grill smashes his knees, as his head collides with

the vehicle's hood. The car hurls his slender frame high into the air, his shoulder bouncing off its windscreen before his limp, lifeless body careers into the concrete floor.

Tyres screech and echo, as the dark sedan turns and races up the exit ramp, leaving the car park otherwise deserted.

The only movement is a constant stream feeding the crimson halo that surrounds the jockey's battered skull.

* * * * * *

Jack Morgan's day begins with a sequence of high pitched beeps from his bedside clock radio. A typical start, for a man forty years a racehorse trainer.

He throws a sheet and two blankets across a sagging mattress and sits up, looking at a photo of his late wife that he keeps in a silver frame on a bedside table.

With a thick mop of greying hair draped over sleep ridden eyes, he stretches his arms above his head, his pyjama jacket riding up to expose a modest torso, yet one quite respectable for a man of sixty three.

He shuffles towards an old wicker chair, buried as it is beneath a pair of crudely patched denim jeans, a faded green polo shirt and navy blue woollen jumper with holes worn in both elbows. He dresses himself, pulling on the second of two leather boots, as a kettle whistles on the stove in the kitchen.

Sally Morgan, twenty-six years Jack's tom boy daughter, lifts the kettle from the stove and pours its contents into three separate cups. She places one on a table in front of a bowl of cereal, rapidly being devoured by seventeen year old stable apprentice Jerry Chapman.

First Tuesday

Richard Harrison

'Morning Dad' Sally says.

'Morning Mr. Morgan' Jerry adds.

'Morning lad' Jack replies and 'Thanks darl' as Sally hands him a cup of black coffee.

He walks over to the window, peels back a curtain and peers outside into a still, dark October morning.

'Rained a bit last night Mr. Morgan' Jerry chirps. 'Reckon the track might cut up a bit.'

'Could do' Jack mutters, sipping from his cup.

The front door of their modest weatherboard swings open and Jack shuffles outside. Sally follows then Jerry, catching the rebounding fly wire on his foot, as he closes the door behind him.

The first ritual of the morning is to load three horses onto their truck, for the five minute commute to the training tracks at Mornington racecourse.

Jack Morgan's three tonne Bedford may be fifteen years old but reliable enough.

Sally walks towards a small stable block, opens each door and warmly greets its tenant. The last horse to be loaded and the first to step off will be the stable's leading light - Star Chaser, a chestnut mare with a white blaze and a gentle temperament. Star Chaser is leased from her breeder, raced in partnership and the best chance Jack will ever have of winning the biggest race on the Australian racing calendar.

Far and above the best horse Jack Morgan has ever trained, Star Chaser followed her victory in the Turnbull Stakes, with a fast finishing fourth in the Caulfield Cup.

She is currently quoted at odds of twelve to one to win

the Melbourne Cup in five days' time.

Sally steps inside the mare's stable.

'Hello Rosie' she whispers, 'leaving for the office again.'

She kneels down and bandages the mare's legs, as Rosie gently nibbles at her pony tail.

Star Chaser is led onto the truck, before Jack swings a rail into position and fastens a bracket.

'Right darl?' he calls to Sally.

'Yep' she replies.

A tug on the rail assures him it is safely fixed in place. He steps off the tailgate and raises it shut.

Sally and Jerry are already sitting in the cabin, as Jack opens the door and lifts himself into the driver's seat.

CHAPTER 2

It is 5.00am when Inspector Frank Dennis arrives in the Crown Casino car park.

Holding a striped, polyester tie to his chest, he ducks under a yellow tape the uniforms have stretched between each of six concrete pillars. The tape defines the area as a CRIME SCENE with the accompanying instruction - DO NOT CROSS.

Crown Casino Public Relations Manager, Tiffany Kirk-Jones has charged herself with the responsibility of convincing the attending media, that what has transpired 'was clearly a dreadful accident.'

The press, completely disinterested in her version of events, are even proving immune to the flirting skills she has spent years honing in the company of the nation's elite sportsmen.

Dennis lifts the corner of a grey blanket, satisfies himself with a glance at the corpse and ushers the ambulance crew away - a white chalk outline defining the spot where the body of superstar jockey and millionaire, Alan Da Silva was found.

The ambulance drives away slowly. There is no need for sirens or haste.

Dennis speaks to the uniformed officers who were first on the scene. There are no witnesses. At least not in the car park. A number of patrons had seen Da Silva leave the casino but none could be sure of the time. The croupier working the $100 minimum Blackjack table figured the time to be around four, as she had begun her shift shortly after three. She reported that Da Silva was alone at the table the whole time she was there, had not spoken to anyone other than a drinks waiter, lost 'a bit' and did not appear to be drunk or upset.

'What do you call a bit?' To lose I mean' Dennis asks.

She thinks for a moment, nervously biting her lip.

'Probably a thousand, fifteen hundred maybe' she says. 'He would win some hands and lose others but overall he would have lost. At least while I was there anyway.'

'Did he say anything before he left?'

She shakes her head.

'Did anyone else leave at the same time or did you see anyone follow him?' Dennis asks.

Nervously she replies 'No' feeling the Inspector is becoming frustrated with her modest input.

'Did you happen to notice if he walked to the escalator straight away? Did he go to the bar, the toilet, did he talk to anyone?' he asks.

'I don't know. I don't think so' she replies.

'You don't think so?' he says.

Shrugging her shoulders, she protests 'I didn't take any

notice. I didn't even know who he was until someone else told me!'

The Inspector thanks her for her time, walks over to Constable Mike Ryan and asks if the statements he and the others had collected can shed any light.

'Not much sir I'm afraid, a couple of car park attendants heard a car racing off, but apparently people speed out of here all the time. They didn't see anything either. People pay to park when they come in and the exit ramp is 100 metres away.'

'Inspector!'

Dennis ignores Tiffany Kirk-Jones as she approaches.

'Inspector!'

'Yes madam' he replies, his eyes roaming the circumference of her bright red and elaborately permed hair.

She extends her hand towards him, several silver bracelets contoured on her wrist.

'Tiffany Kirk-Jones Inspector. I am the Media Director for the casino.'

Dennis shakes her hand, noting her shocking pink nail polish and striking olive complexion.

He greets her, reluctantly.

'How do you do' he says.

Kirk-Jones holds her hands together. She touches both index fingers to her chin, as if in deep thought and gestures to the policeman.

'Inspector, may I ask, before you might make any statement to the press, just what you have concluded thus far.'

Dennis stands with his hands buried in his pockets.

'Not a great deal at this stage madam. The body was discovered shortly after four o'clock. The injuries the victim suffered are entirely consistent with him being struck by a motor vehicle at some speed. A car was heard driving off at the time the incident occurred, but at this stage we do not have any witnesses.'

'And are you treating it as an accident. I mean clearly…'

'Madam' he interrupts. 'I am not treating it as anything at this stage. Tell me, we believe the deceased is in fact the famous jockey Alan Da Silva, Who I am told is a friend and associate of Mr. Maressmo.'

Kirk-Jones responds.

'Yes indeed' she says, 'and I can assure you that my employer is very upset. As indeed we all are Inspector.'

Chapter 3

A slim, attractive female appears around the corner of the stables at the Mornington racecourse. It is dark, but unmistakably Sally Morgan. She is leading a relaxed and languid Star Chaser.

Ahead, leaning on a rail dividing two stables and sipping coffee from a paper cup, is Tommy Holt.

'What took you so long?' he says smiling. 'I got here from Melbourne ahead of you. You've only got to come 5 minutes.'

Sally smiles, as Jerry and Jack coax two three year old geldings off the float, leading them through the gate.

Sally walks Star Chaser into her stall, as Tommy steps back, lifting his skull cap and whip out of the way.

'G'day Jack' he calls out, looking past the young apprentice in the process.

'Tommy,' Jack says.

Jack Morgan has long regarded jockeys a necessary evil, quick to take credit but slow to assume responsibility. All the same Tommy Holt had demonstrated a tremendous affinity with Star Chaser and when it comes to winning big races (not something Jack Morgan has a habit of doing), it will pay to have him aboard.

With each horse safely housed in its stall, Sally and Jerry walk back to the truck to fetch all the gear, as Tommy runs his hand down the mare's neck.

'She looks well Jack' he says. 'Ready to peak at three o'clock next Tuesday I reckon.'

'That's the plan' Jack mutters.

Jerry returns, he swings a bag off his shoulder and drops it on the ground at Mr. Morgan's feet. Jack unzips it and pulls out a leather bridle.

He encourages a bit into the mare's mouth, resting the reins on her wither, as Sally helps to fit a saddle in place.

Tommy thrusts his cup towards Jerry, spilling its contents over his hands and shirt. He dons his cap and climbs onto the mare's back, fitting his toes in each stirrup.

Jack takes a pair of binoculars out of the bag, as he and Sally follow Star Chaser out to the track. Jerry fills two buckets with water and rushes to catch them up.

Tommy holds the mare up at the entry to the track - a four metre gap in the running rail, as Jack calls out.

'Just let her trot a lap to warm up, then I want you to do 2,000 evens, letting her come home the last 400.'

'Righto' Tommy calls back.

Jack, Sally and Jerry step up onto a platform to watch.

Tommy does exactly as instructed, trotting the mare a lap of the course, before maintaining a three quarter pace of fifteen seconds to the furlong.

As they approach the 400 metre mark, Jack feels for a

stop watch in his pocket. With one hand training his binoculars on the mare, he flicks his watch with the other.

The clock ticks as the mare quickens. Tommy pushes her along for a handful of strides, letting her finish the gallop off at her own pace. As they race past, Jack clicks his watch to a stop. Tommy drops his hands and eases her down.

'How did she do Dad?' Sally asks.

'Twenty four and a half' he says.

Tommy trots Star Chaser back and meets Jack at her stall.

'Sweet as a nut Jack' he says, dragging the saddle from her back. 'Travelled beautifully and when I asked her, she took hold of the bit and worked really nice.'

'Yeah, she went well' Jack responds, bending down to run his hands over the mare's knees.

Tommy calls out 'Alright then mate, I'll see you tomorrow' as he jogs to his car.

Jack and Jerry saddle the two three year olds; Up and Over and Hit Musical - two geldings that 'can't get within ten lengths of Star Chaser' but might be able to pick up a race or two in the bush all the same.

Sally climbs aboard Up and Over, while Jack legs Jerry onto Hit Musical.

Jack barks his instructions.

'Trot one, then do 1600 evens, coming home the last six. And try to keep them together.'

The riders head off, as two paramedics walk across the track, towards an ambulance parked on the inside of the course.

'Beat us here again' one calls out.

'Gotta get first use of it' Jack says.

The rules stipulate that no horse can be worked on the course unless an ambulance is on standby, but no one ever seemed to mind that old Jack was out a bit early.

The first ray of sunlight flicks across the course as Jack mounts the platform again, dreaming of what might come next Tuesday. His mind traces back to when Sally's mother was alive, to the many fifteen hundred dollar yearlings he broke in, trained and sent around in low grade maiden events, hoping to pick up a win for a handful of local owners to brag about in the pub.

For the first time in his life he has a chance at the big time, a chance to measure up to the likes of Lewis, Harper and Woolley, the supposed training elite, and all this with just three horses in work on a modest six acre property.

Sally and Jerry come trotting into the straight aboard the two three year olds, passing a row of sponsor marquees, still standing from the previous day's meeting, when a gust of wind blows a colourful sign across the track in front of them. Both horses take fright and rear in the air. Sally is able to control Up and Over, but Jerry's mount lurches sideways, tipping him out of the saddle and spearing him into the turf.

Hit Musical, suddenly free of his rider, confused and frightened, clenches the bit in his teeth and bolts. Jack drops his binoculars and makes for the gap in the rail. If the horse gets through there, he could end up on the road and its only 200 metres to the highway.

Jack stands in the middle of the gap, as the riderless Hit

Musical heads straight for it. With arms stretched wide apart, he creeps forward, reins flapping at the horse's side, its head held high at a full gallop.

His heart pounding, Jack pleads 'Whoa boy, whoa!' as the horse's chest crashes into his own. His body is thrown back, narrowly missing both the edge of the rail and the platform.

Hit Musical changes direction and bolts freely around the track, as Jack Morgan lies unconscious on the ground.

The ambulance crew win the race to be first on the scene.

A paramedic kneels over Jack's body, as Sally arrives aboard Up and Over. Jerry Chapman is sprinting but still a furlong out.

'Dad are you okay!?' Sally cries, as it is confirmed her father is still breathing.

'Is he alright?' she pleads.

'Well he took one hell of a knock, I can tell you that much' a paramedic says.

'What idiot left all that crap lying around? What do we do?' Sally says.

'Stretcher' the paramedic shouts, 'Dave!'

Dave runs to the ambulance, as his partner reassures Sally.

'I'm sure he'll be fine' he says, 'but he is unconscious, so we will whip him off to hospital and they can have a look at him.'

Jerry Chapman, desperately short of breath, falls to his knees beside them.

'Oh shit Sally, I'm so sorry' he says, panting furiously. 'He just threw me off.'

'It's alright' she says, putting her hand on the boy's arm. 'Take this horse back and try to catch yours okay.'

Jerry bounces to his feet, determined to do what he can to make good.

'Right' he says, gulping air into his lungs, as he takes Up and Over's reins and jogs with him back to the stables.

Jack's neck is fitted with a brace.

'Just a precaution' Sally is told, as Jack is lifted onto a stretcher and loaded into the back of the ambulance.

'Where will you take him?' she asks, 'Frankston?'

'Right away' they say, as the doors slam shut.

Chapter 4

Sally drives the truck back to the property, with all three horses aboard. Both she and Jerry having spent some time catching the wayward Hit Musical.

With Star Chaser safely back in her stable, she lists the duties Jerry will need to complete on his own, as she will be going straight to the hospital.

As the last horse steps off the truck, she calls out. 'Now are you right?! Do you know what to do?!'

'I'm good!' Jerry calls back, fearful of the condition Sally will find her father in when she does finally reach the hospital.

Sally runs into the house, lifts her keys from a table and a mobile phone from the kitchen bench. The front door slams shut, as she jogs towards her hatchback.

'I've got the phone if you need me!' she shouts, the wheels of her car spinning two bare patches in the gravel driveway.

Sally races down the slope, telling herself to both calm and slow down. One serious injury a matter of days away from the most important day of their lives is trouble enough.

She turns the radio off and the corners in third, reaching the highway in record time.

She arrives at the hospital, jogs from the car park and approaches two women standing behind a large reception desk.

'Excuse me' she says, looking at each in turn.

One of the women looks up and walks towards her.

'Can I help you?' she says.

Sally explains that her father would have arrived by ambulance from the racecourse about an hour ago.

The woman sits down in front of a computer. She taps at the keyboard and hits the return button three times.

She looks up from the screen.

'I'll get one of the doctors to speak with you' she says.

Sally protests. 'Is he alright?'

'I'm sorry' she says, 'I'll have to get a doctor.'

She suggests Sally sits down, then picks up a telephone and turns her back.

Sally flops in a chair and watches the two women sort more folders.

A young, male doctor walks across to the woman Sally had spoken to minutes before. He looks over, relishing the opportunity to offer some comfort to the concerned and attractive female.

'Hello, I'm Doctor Collier' he says.

Sally shakes his hand.

'We've got your Dad staying with us' he says with a smile.

'Is he alright?' Sally asks nervously.

'Well, not entirely' he says, 'I understand he got cleaned up by a runaway horse?'

'Something like that' Sally says.

Realising his desire to impress her has fallen woefully short, the doctor's manner becomes more factual.

'Well he was knocked unconscious, but came to in the ambulance on the way here, so that's good' he says.

Sally breathes more easily, as the doctor continues.

'We took some X –Rays of his chest and shoulder and also did what's called a CT scan' he says. 'He has a compound fracture, just below the shoulder, and a couple of cracked ribs.'

'So what does that mean?' Sally says.

'Well, he's lucky that we have an orthopaedic guy here at the moment, otherwise we would have had to send him up to Melbourne.'

'Orthopaedic?' Sally asks.

'We need to operate to repair the shoulder. I dare say he'll probably need a couple of screws in there. In fact…' he says looking at his watch. 'He's being prepped for surgery now.'

Sally raises a trembling hand to her face. 'He's being operated on?'

'Yes he is' the doctor says. It will be a few hours at least I should think. You are welcome to wait here or we can give you a call at home or at work.'

Sally sighs, holds her hands behind her head and tries to collect her thoughts.

'I'll wait here' she says.

The doctor points to a vending machine, if she 'should feel like a cup of coffee' and assures her that someone will come by and look after her.

Sally slouches in a chair, folds her arms, waits and worries.

The environment of Frankston Hospital is all too familiar. Little has changed in the three short years since she last visited her mother here. Three years since bowel cancer stole her best friend and left her father a widower.

She takes a mobile phone from the pocket of her jeans, calls her employer at the photo and print shop in Hastings, to apologise and explain her absence.

Two newspapers, three magazines, a cup of hot chocolate and four hours later, another doctor speaks to her.

Doctor Westlake tells her that notwithstanding the fact her father's shoulder 'was a bit of a mess' the operation had gone well. Two cracked ribs had not punctured his lungs and a subsequent X –Ray had confirmed the fact three screws and a foot of wire now held his shoulder together.

Sally could see her father shortly, but as he has only just come around, she should not expect too much by way of conversation.

She sits down again before a short, plump nurse invites her to visit.

Sally skips up a set of stairs and along a succession of corridors, struggling to keep pace with her quick stepping escort.

Sister Speedy opens the door to Ward - West 2, pointing past two other patients, various visitor chairs, curtain screens, drips and pulleys, to a bed where her father lies propped against three pillows.

Sally feels a lump in her throat and puts a hand over her mouth.

Her father was in a bad way when he lay unconscious at

the track early in the day, but he looks even worse now. His face is pale and swollen, his mouth dry and cracked and his left arm and chest is buried beneath a mass of bandages and tape. He looks as though Hit Musical knocked him down and someone reversed over him in the truck.

Sally sits next to her father's bed, resting her hand on his arm, careful not to disturb the drip stuck in his wrist.

'Hi Dad, are you okay?' she whispers.

Her father lifts a finger and taps his blanket.

'Everything's fine Dad' she says. 'The horses are great. They've all eaten up, the boxes have been mucked out and we will walk them this afternoon.'

Jack nods his head. His dry, parched lips slowly prise apart, as he whispers 'Right.'

Sally teases him about his 'flash new pyjamas' a standard smock, draped across his chest and tied at the back. Only one arm is intact enough to fit through the sleeve.

She explains how Hit Musical shied, threw Jerry off, bolted and knocked him down. That it wasn't the boy's fault. She reminds him that Tommy Holt galloped Star Chaser, how she floated over the ground, that nothing will beat her next Tuesday and how nice it would be if Mum was still alive and she could be there too.

Sally sits by her father's bed for an hour, reminiscing of horses and races and holidays at the beach. She cries as he holds her hand.

3.20pm and Sally leaves the hospital with none of the haste with which she arrived. She makes her way back home, passing the Chapman's corner store on the way. Jerry's father is standing outside the shop, inserting a headline poster for the Herald Sun PM edition into a wire display cage.

Sally reads the copy, pulls over and jumps out of the car.

The headline, printed in large, black capital letters reads;

CUP JOCKEY SLAIN IN CASINO HIT AND RUN

CHAPTER 5

'Hi Fred' Sally says.

Fred Chapman looks up from a neat row of display cages, raising his hand to shield his eyes from the sun.

'Hello Sally' he says warmly.

'Just want to grab a paper' she says, pushing open the shop door.

A small bell tinkles, as Fred calls out 'Of course. By the way, did you see…?

Sally picks up the newspaper.

The front page features the headline, SUPERSTAR JOCKEY SLAIN, above three colour photographs and an article that 'continues on page three.'

The first photo shows a beaming Alan Da Silva, unsaddling another big race winner and generating his signature 'V' for victory gesture. The second is a shot taken in the car park of Crown Casino. Presumably, the lump strapped to a stretcher and hidden under a grey blanket is Alan Da Silva. The third had been taken a week ago. It shows Lord Melbery, the 4 to 1 favourite for the Melbourne Cup, being led back to scale after winning the W.S. Cox Plate. Da

Silva is in the saddle, standing high in the irons and waving his whip to the crowd. The horse is being led by its owner, Albert Maressmo. A caption running underneath the photo reads; 'Who will ride the Cup favourite now?'

'That's a bit of a shock, isn't it?' Fred says, looking over Sally's shoulder, as she opens the paper to page three.

'I'll say' she says, her eyes scanning the text.

'How's your Dad?' Fred asks.

'Oh he's...'

Sally is so engrossed in the drama surrounding Alan Da Silva, she forgets for the moment that her father is lying in a post-operative hospital bed, his smashed shoulder secured by screws and wire.

'Actually, he's not the best Fred' she says. 'We had an accident at the track this morning. One of the three year olds got loose and knocked him down, busted his shoulder.'

Sally looks up from the newspaper, neglecting to tell Fred that his son had been riding the culprit moments before.

'Oh my God!' Fred says, 'that's terrible. Where is he now?'

'Hospital' Sally says, 'Frankston. They had to operate to repair his shoulder. He snapped the top bit of his arm clean off.'

Fred raises both hands in mock surrender. 'Oh no, for goodness sake, spare me the details' he says. 'I hate all that stuff. Will he be okay?'

'He'll be right Fred' she says, 'tough as old boots my Dad.'

Sally smiles, as the colour returns to Fred's face.

'What are you going to do with the horses then? What about Star Chaser? Everyone around here is so excited. You'd reckon they all owned a share!' he says.

'We'll be okay Fred' Sally says. 'Take more than that to knock us around.'

She folds the paper under her arm, takes some change from her pocket and hands it to him.

'Better go' she says, passing a stack of biscuits and instant coffee on her way to the door.

Fred calls after her. 'How's Jerry going? Is he alright?'

'Good as gold Fred!' she calls back, as the shop door closes behind her.

It is almost four o'clock and time to get home, walk all of the horses, feed up and check to see if Jerry is indeed as good as gold. Sally starts her car, pulls out onto the highway and makes a mental note to ring Star Chaser's owner John O'Connor.

Her car reaches the top of the driveway, where she can see the tip of a broom sweeping back and forth. Jerry Chapman is attached to it, generating a pile of straw and dust on an otherwise spotless slab of concrete.

He leans the broom against a wall and walks over to the car, waiting to gauge by Sally's face, just how grim his future might be. If Mr. Morgan is dead, a clean stable floor and a collection of saddles you can see your reflection in, isn't likely to save him.

Jerry is too afraid to speak. He stands with his hands by his sides.

'He'll live' Sally says, with a smile that buckles the boy's knees.

Jerry reaches forward to hug her, but thinks better of it, brushing his hands on his trousers in an effort to disguise his original intent.

Sally laughs, wraps her arm around his shoulders and ruffles his hair as Jerry sighs with relief.

He's a bit banged up but he'll be alright' she says.

CHAPTER 6

Jerry kicks off his boots, pushes the door open and shuffles into the kitchen. His socks, damp with perspiration, leave a trail of moisture on the tiled floor.

Sally has left the newspaper lying face up on the kitchen table, as she fills the kettle.

Jerry peels off a woollen sweater and leans over the front page.

'Crikey' he says. 'Who are they going to get to ride it now?'

'You should give them a call Jerry. Len Lewis' number is in the calendar' Sally says smiling. 'Give Albert Maressmo a bell while you're at it.'

She points to a telephone that hangs next to a cork notice board, thick with business cards for feed merchants, farriers and vets.

'Of course' Sally says, 'If you want to pass up the chance to ride the favourite in the Melbourne Cup, that's your business.'

Jerry holds his left hand to his ear, extending his thumb and little finger.

'Hello Mr. Lewis, its Jerry Chapman here.'

'Who?'

'Jerry Chapman, Mr. Lewis. I'm an apprentice jockey sir and I was wondering if I could ride Lord Melbery for you on Tuesday. What's that? Qualified? Mr. Lewis I'll have you know that I haven't fallen off one since, hmm, let me see, I think it was this morning!'

Jerry mimes the act of hanging up the phone.

'Who was that on the phone Len?' he mimics.

'Oh some bloke called Johnny Chapstick. Circus performer I think, falls off horses for a living apparently.'

Sally doesn't tease him again.

'Anyway' she says, 'Things could be worse. You could be Alan Da Silva, lying under a sheet in the morgue.'

'That's true' he says, adding 'So when does Mr. Morgan get out of hospital?'

'I think in a day or two, but we can go and see him tonight after dinner. He'll have to tell us what he wants us to do in the morning anyway.'

'Tonight?' Jerry says. 'Do you want me come?'

Sally chuckles to herself. 'Don't worry he's not going to bite you. Anyway, he couldn't catch you if he tried.'

For the next two hours, Sally and Jerry follow their afternoon routine, walking each of the horses along the roads and tracks surrounding the property.

By six o'clock all the horses have returned to their stables to be fed and watered.

Sally heats up a leftover stir-fry in the microwave, when the television news leads with the story of Alan Da Silva's death.

She walks into the lounge room and sits on the edge of the couch next to Jerry. They watch glued to the screen, as the footage cuts from Crown Casino's elaborate signage, to the basement car park, to Lord Melbery winning the Cox Plate.

There is a statement from the policeman heading the investigation. His name super imposed at the base of the screen - Inspector Frank Dennis. He and his colleagues 'are following numerous lines of enquiry.'

The Inspector's moment in the spotlight is followed by a serious and stern Tiffany Kirk-Jones, lamenting 'the tragic demise of a wonderful sportsman, a great loss to the nation and a very distressing time for everyone involved with the casino.'

'My God!' Sally cries, 'what's with the hair. It looks like her head's on fire.'

Jerry chuckles, as Sally walks into the kitchen responding to the beeping microwave.

Trainer Len Lewis is interviewed and asked who will now ride Lord Melbery in the Melbourne Cup?

'Jerry Chapman!' is the call from the couch.

Lewis appears relaxed and confident. The weather is overcast and the light dim, yet his eyes are concealed by dark sunglasses. He is standing outside his stable complex, as horses and handlers stroll nonchalantly behind.

'Well firstly, let me say how upset everyone connected with the stable is. Alan was a tremendous jockey and a great bloke. He will be sorely missed. As far as who will ride the horse, I have spoken with Mr. Maressmo this afternoon and we expect to finalise an engagement by tomorrow morning.'

'And how is Lord Melbery?' a reporter asks.

Grinning, he replies 'Jumping out of his skin.'

'Jumping out of his skin, but without a rider?' the reporter confirms.

'Lewis, folds his arms across his chest. 'In time' he says and walks out of shot.

Jerry calls out to the kitchen. 'They haven't said who's going to ride Lord Melbery yet.'

'So you're still a chance then' Sally says cheekily. 'Better leave the answering machine on when we go out.

Chapter 7

Sister Speedy takes a tray from the table suspended above bed number three in ward West 4.

'We should have given you a big, tough piece of steak Mr. Morgan. That would be a bit of a challenge to eat with one hand' she says.

'Reckon so' Jack says, as he leans back, squeezing three pillows against the frame of his bed.

Speedy slots his tray, plates and cutlery into a stainless steel trolley and wheels the table away from the side of the bed, as Sally, Jerry and a large quantity of jelly beans enter the ward.

'Come to see the one armed bandit' the nurse says.

Sally smiles and walks over to her father's bed. Jerry trails a few feet behind.

'Hi Sal' he says. 'I see you brought Teflon with you.'

'Teflon' stands behind Sally. The jelly beans his parents had given him for Mr. Morgan are wrapped in yellow, white and black ribbons. Jack Morgan's racing colours, the colours Star Chaser will carry next Tuesday.

'I'm sorry Mr. Morgan' he says, presenting the jar in both hands.

29

Jack beckons the boy towards him.

Jerry slides along the side of the bed, handing the jar to Sally.

'Here' Jack says, raising his arm in the air.

Jerry moves closer, as Sally looks on.

Jack drops his arm and lays it across the boy's back. He grips his neck and looks him in the eye.

'Now listen to me' he says. 'It wasn't your fault. It was an accident. So don't you go around feeling sorry for yourself, you just do whatever Sally asks you to do okay? We've got a race to win.'

'Yes sir' Jerry says, feeling like a convicted felon, let off with a stern warning by a kind hearted magistrate.

'You're looking a lot better Dad' Sally says, holding up the jar. 'These are from Fred and Beryl. We thought you could exercise your good arm digging out all the black ones.'

'Good idea' he says, before asking Jerry to fetch a couple of chairs.

'Anyway, you wouldn't have heard the big news' Sally says.

'What? Da Silva?' he says.

'So you are up to speed then?' Sally says.

'I heard it on the news. That joker over there had it on before' he says, pointing to the back of a small television set, standing at the foot of a bed occupied by an elderly man, asleep with a plastic tube taped to the inside of his nose.

'So what do you reckon?' she asks.

'Dunno. Word is he used to gamble a lot. Apparently used to punt like nothing on earth' Jack says.

'Really? So do you think it was an accident?' Sally wonders.

'Probably not' Jack says. 'Anyone who is mixed up with that Maressmo character has got to be bad news. He was thick as all hell with him, always at the casino and look where it got him.'

'Even Tommy Holt has some sort of sponsorship arrangement with Crown' Sally says.

'Most of them do' Jack says.

'Anyway you'll have to get in touch with a few people' he says. 'John O'Connor for one, though he'll probably ring anyway, you had better give him a bell, tell him everything will be fine. That'll make his day if you call him up' Jack says, clutching at the pain in his shoulder.

'Ah, serves you right' Sally says.

'When is he going to ask you out anyway? I'll grow old and die waiting for the day' Jack says.

'Don't be ridiculous' Sally says, 'he's almost as old as you!'

'And he lives with his mother' Jack says.

'Seriously?!' Sally says.

'No he doesn't' Jack says, 'at least I don't think he does.'

'Perhaps he's just waiting for you to drop off the perch first' Sally says.

'Well we came close enough this morning didn't we?' Jack says. 'They showed me the X-Rays they took before and after the operation. Fair dinkum, the top of my arm came clean off. It was hanging down here!'

Jack exaggerates, indicating a point half way between his shoulder and elbow.

31

'Now I've got a couple of bloody great screws and all this wire in there. I told them they're not coming out to our place to fix any of the fences. It all looked pretty shabby to me.'

'So what's the go in the morning Dad?' Sally asks.

'Well Star Chaser won't need anything more than gentle pace work, so tell Tommy to hold her together. I only want her to canter 2000 metres half pace.'

'Got it' Sally says.

Jack lists the work each horse should be given. Sally listens intently, as Jerry takes notes.

'Can you handle the truck alright?' he asks.

Sally leans back in her chair, offended at the suggestion, but smiling all the same.

'What do you reckon?' she says.

Her father raises a hand in apology.

'I just want to know everything is okay that's all.'

'Everything's fine Dad' Sally says. 'Everything's fine.'

CHAPTER 8

Frank Dennis drops a set of keys on a small timber table and closes the door of his modest two bedroom flat.

He walks into the kitchen, opens a cupboard and takes out a bottle of Scotch. He carries it into the lounge, flops in a chair and pours himself a drink.

A leaflet with the headline 'When it stops being fun, walk away' acts as a coaster.

He tosses the contents of his glass down his throat, pours himself another and lights a cigarette.

Slouched in his chair he glances up at a bookshelf, his eyes scanning a faded, dog eared scrap book. Its dank, yellowing pages host a plethora of press clippings from the Herald, Sun and Age newspapers. Articles and photographs that chronicle the short but spectacular career of an outstanding apprentice jockey, a young man possessed of choir boy looks and an impish grin, together with extraordinary balance, tremendous strength and an uncommon affinity with race horses.

The boy's career began at sixteen, peaking when Exalted saluted the judge in the Toorak Handicap, a week before winning the Caulfield Cup.

It ended three years, six inches and several kilograms later, when increasing weight forced him out of the saddle, though the drinking and gambling continued.

Frank Dennis could have been anything as a jockey and for a time he was. A gifted and brilliant rider, he was an idol to some and the envy of many.

Eventually opportunities simply dried up. The phone stopped ringing and before long it became a choice between the police and the army.

Today, some thirty years on, he reflects on what might have been.

CHAPTER 9

A telephone rings in the hallway of a renovated, Victorian terrace. A row of framed race finish photographs hangs on the wall, as a forty seven year old accountant picks up the handset.

'Hello, John O'Connor' he says.

'Hello John, Sally Morgan' a voice replies.

'Hi Sally' he says excitedly, 'How are you?'

'Fine thanks. You?' she says.

'Well I can't wait for next Tuesday for one thing' he says. 'How's the champ, is she okay?'

'She's fine' Sally confirms.

'Working well, eating up, looking a million dollars?' he asks.

'All of the above' she says.

O'Connor loosens his tie, undoes his top button and leans with his hand pressed against the wall.

'Actually I'm ringing to tell you that Dad is in hospital?' Sally says.

'Oh my God! You're kidding! What's happened?' he asks.

'He was knocked down at the track this morning' she

says. 'One of the three year olds bolted and he tried to stop it getting out onto the road. Smashed his shoulder and broke a couple of ribs in the process.'

'Bloody hell' John says. 'What do we do? What can I do?'

'Nothing' Sally says. 'It's okay. He's given Jerry and me all the instructions and Tommy Holt will be down to ride your mare in the morning. He should be home in a day or two and we will just have to do the best we can.'

'Well if I can do anything, let me know. I'll drive down in the morning if it will help. I can take the day off work.'

Sally laughs. 'Tomorrow's Saturday dummy.'

'Well easier still' he says.

'It's okay John' she says, 'we will be pretty busy and going back and forth to see Dad I imagine, but thanks all the same.'

Sally puts the handset down moments before the phone rings. It is Tommy Holt.

'Hello Tommy' she says, 'What about Da Silva then?'

'Yeah, shocking' he says, with none of the emotion and concern she expected. 'Can I speak to Jack?'

'Afraid not' Sally says. 'He's lying in a hospital bed with a busted shoulder. I guess Da Silva's demise is bigger news than that, otherwise we might have made the front page.'

'When did that happen?' he asks.

'This morning, not long after you left. One threw the kid off and bolted. It's okay though we will be there tomorrow.'

'So has he got a mobile I can reach him on?' Tommy asks.

'No. Why? Is there a problem?' Sally says.

'I really need to speak to Jack' he says.

'Well you might be able to stop in and see him in the morning' she says, 'I'm not sure how the hospital…'

Tommy interrupts, 'I can't come down in the morning.'

Sally is both surprised and concerned.

'Oh, well I guess that's okay, Dad reckons she just…'

He interrupts again.

'And I can't ride your horse in the Cup' he says.

CHAPTER 10

Sally drops her back against the notice board. She slides down the wall and sits on the floor, the handset pressed against her ear.

Tommy Holt has switched his mount for the Melbourne Cup. He will ride for Len Lewis and Albert Maressmo. He will ride Lord Melbery.

'I'm sorry Sally' he says.

'You can't simply jump off her' Sally protests. 'You made a commitment!'

'I know. But there is more to it than that' he says.

'No there isn't. There's nothing more to it at all' she says.

'Sally listen, and whatever you do don't repeat this to anyone. Not even your Dad okay. Maressmo had Da Silva killed.'

'That's ridiculous' she says. 'Why on earth would he murder the jockey who is riding his own horse, the favourite for God's sake, in a Melbourne Cup.'

'Sally, you remember last year' he says, 'when Break of Day won the Cup and Maressmo took millions from the bookies.'

'He's supposed to have ruined a couple.' she says.

'Yeah, well Da Silva is on Bridal Waltz okay. Starts favourite, gets a mile out of its ground, settles near last and flies home to run fifth. Do you reckon he was trying? Hell no. And he had plenty of mates too' he says. 'Maressmo has got the best form students and professional punters in the country working for him. They tell him the main chances, he pays off the jocks and they manage to get beat. It's as simple as that.'

'In a Melbourne Cup!' she shouts. 'Don't be stupid!'

'Well for a start, it's about the only race all year where the bookies hold enough money to stand the amounts he bets and you have got no idea how much he paid them.'

'Them or us?' she asks

Holt doesn't answer as Sally continues.

'Anyway, that doesn't explain…'

Holt interrupts.

'Yeah well Da Silva's a cocky prick and he's got a big mouth. At least he did anyway. Word was getting out.'

'So?' Sally says.

'So you don't mess with Maressmo. He's a mad bastard. He's hooked up with the mafia. He had one of his goons knock Da Silva off, just to shut him and everyone else up' he says 'in his own bloody car park for Christ's sake!'

'And you're going to ride for him?' Sally says.

'I have to' he says.

'Why?' Sally says, 'because you pulled one up last year as well?'

'Look I'm sorry okay' Holt says.

Sally thrusts the handset into the cradle. She looks across to see Jerry standing in the doorway.

'You okay?' he asks.

'Not really' she says.

'Why did he jump off her anyway?' Jerry asks.

'I don't know' Sally says.

'Are you going to tell your Dad?' Jerry asks.

'Not unless you want to' she says.

'Not particularly' he says.

Jerry retreats to the lounge room, sits in a chair and stares at the television.

Sally stands in the kitchen and contemplates telling her father that their jockey has just sacked Star Chaser so he can ride Lord Melbery. She thinks of lodging a complaint with the stewards and forcing Tommy Holt to honour his commitment. But then Star Chaser misses the start and drifts back in a twenty four horse field. She settles in a hopeless position, storming home when the race is all over to miss a place. Tommy Holt tells her father how she got unbalanced at the start, on her wrong leg going out of the straight the first time, raced too keenly, jarred up on the hard track, was disappointed for a run, got off the bit early and couldn't get a clear run until it was too late.

There is always plenty of trouble and interference in a big field - especially if you go out of your way to find it.

CHAPTER 11

Friday night and thousands of punters are gathered in Crown Casino. Most mill around a myriad of gambling pits, governed by croupiers in uniformed waistcoats, while others perch on stools facing rows of warbling poker machines.

Inspector Frank Dennis wanders among them. A quiet and inconspicuous observer, as '17 Black' extracts a boisterous cheer from a nearby roulette table.

He watches a pile of chips slide across the table, lovingly embraced by a Chinese man smoking a cigarette, when a voice interrupts.

'Any luck Inspector?'

Dennis turns around to see Tiffany Kirk-Jones, she with the hair and fingernails.

'Most of it bad' he says.

'Roulette Inspector?' she says. 'I would have thought you more of a blackjack man. More considered and calculating.'

'Not on my salary' he says.

'Yes quite. Tell me, how is your investigation progressing? Have you managed to uncover anything of note?'

'Not really, but as you are here, perhaps I could ask you a few questions' he says.

'Why certainly. Only too happy to co-operate' she says smiling.

She invites the Inspector to the Mahogany Room, an exclusive section of the casino reserved for 'members' and so called 'high rollers.'

They sit down either side of a small table and order a round of drinks - white wine for her and lemonade for him.

'So how long have you worked for the casino madam?' he asks.

'Since we opened Inspector and please, it's Tiffany or Miss, at the very least.'

'Right' Dennis mutters, spying Tommy Holt sitting at a blackjack table in the company of a tall, leggy blonde.

Kirk-Jones turns around but does not respond.

'Miss' Dennis says, 'I was curious to learn that Alan Da Silva and one or two other jockeys for that matter, enjoy quite a flexible line of credit with the casino. What can you tell me about that?'

The PR Manager sits back in her chair and folds her arms across her chest.

'Inspector, I'm sure you can appreciate, arrangements of that nature are entirely confidential' she says.

'No doubt' Dennis says, 'but as I understand it, Da Silva was granted a $100,000 credit facility that he never repaid, and in fact he had run up losses of two or three times that amount.'

'I don't see the point you are trying to make Inspector'

Kirk-Jones says, 'but all the same, I'm simply not privy to the nature of what are essentially private arrangements.'

'When you say private, you mean these are arrangements brokered by Mr. Maressmo himself?' Dennis says.

'Absolutely Inspector' she says 'but by the same token, I cannot imagine for one moment that Mr. Da Silva's financial arrangements with the casino could possibly have anything to do with this whole dreadful business.'

'I'm not suggesting they do Miss' Dennis says, 'I'm simply trying to establish a motive.'

'Well far be it from me Inspector' she says, 'but have you considered some of his rival jockeys, even trainers and owners for that matter? He was riding the favourite in a Melbourne Cup after all. Perhaps it was simply opportunism or envy.'

'Perhaps it was' Dennis says, as Tommy Holt plants a kiss on his partner's cheek.

"Will that be all Inspector?' the PR Manager says, as she stands. 'I really must be moving on.'

Dennis nods. 'That's fine. Thank you' he says.

Tiffany Kirk-Jones walks away, as the policeman casts an eye towards the blackjack table.

A tall dark haired man dressed in a suit leans down and whispers in Tommy Holt's ear, ushering him away, as his partner juggles a hundred dollar chip between her fingers.

Dennis walks across. He takes Holt's seat at the table, handing $200 in cash to the croupier in return for ten $20 chips.

'Any luck?' he quips to the tall blonde on his left.

'Not much' she mutters, sipping from her glass.

Five minutes and nine hands later, Dennis clenches his left fist above his knee, while his right fumbles for his wallet.

Just then, Tommy Holt returns, placing his hand on his partner's shoulder whispering 'Gotta go babe?'

Dennis swings around in his chair, presenting his Police ID saying 'Before you do. Perhaps I could have a word.'

The three of them retire to the same table, where Dennis had spoken with Tiffany Kirk-Jones, minutes before.

'Nasty business with your colleague' Dennis says.

'I'll say' Holt replies, adding 'we were good friends.'

'Rivals though' Dennis suggests.

'Friends first' Holt confirms, as his partner stands and walks towards the toilets.

'Look' he says, 'I don't know what you are trying to suggest Inspector but I am as shocked and upset as anyone.'

'I am sure you are' Dennis says, and I am sorry for your loss but all the same, to the best of your knowledge, did Da Silva have a gambling problem or debts of any significance?'

'Nah' Holt says, shaking his head.

Dennis continues, 'Had anyone made any threats against him, had he upset the wrong people, big punters for example?'

'Mate, he was at the top of his game' Holt protests. 'He was riding winners, left, right and centre, for all the best trainers and making a fortune in the process.'

'Not any more he isn't' Dennis says.

Holt sighs 'No.'

'What about his relationship with Albert Maressmo?' Dennis asks.

'What about it?' Holt replies.

'Cordial, respectful, successful' Dennis says.

'All of the above' Holt says. 'He's been riding for him for years.'

'Perhaps, but it's my understanding that he owed the casino two, perhaps three hundred thousand dollars.' Dennis suggests, 'What do you know about that?'

Holt laughs it off. 'He could have made that much tomorrow, Tuesday at the latest.'

'So you have no idea who or indeed why anyone would want to see him dead?' Dennis says.

Holt shrugs his shoulders. 'Haven t got a clue' he says.

'People tell me that you will be riding Lord Melbery in the Cup now' Dennis says.

'Oh hell' Holt protests, 'you are not going to start pointing the finger at me!'

'No' Dennis says. 'Good luck. That's all.'

CHAPTER 12

Sally wrestles the Bedford into the car park, behind the Mornington racecourse.

It is 5.00am Saturday, and the car park is largely empty. She looks around, in case Tommy Holt's BMW is in the vicinity. It isn't. The reality is Star Chaser, the horse on the fourth line of betting for Tuesday's Melbourne Cup, is without a confirmed rider.

Oblivious to any drama, the mare looks down at the truck's sloping tail, satisfies herself that it is safely in position and steps off. Jerry takes the three year old Up and Over from the adjoining bay and hands a lead to Sally, as she walks both horses through the gate at the back of the course.

With all three horses unloaded and stabled, including the villainous Hit Musical, Jerry helps to prepare the mare.

He unbuckles the stirrups, dons a skull cap and clips it under his chin. Sally hoists him into the saddle, as he picks up the reins and walks Star Chaser through the gap in the rail where his boss lay unconscious the previous day.

Sally untangles her father's binoculars, from a bag and walks towards the platform.

She focuses on the mare, as she canters around the back of the course and imagines her passing Flemington's 800 metre mark, easing away from the rail and starting to make a run.

Just then, rival trainer Bill Meeks steps onto the platform.

'How's old Jack?' he says, 'I hear he's going to be okay.'

'He's broken his arm and cracked a couple of ribs' Sally says, 'but he'll live.'

'Not long now then.' Meeks says 'The whole town's excited. I reckon a thousand will go just from here.'

Sally lowers her binoculars and smiles.

No pressure then' she says.

'Yeah, he's well liked your Dad. You know there's a lot of jealousy in this game but I reckon everyone wants to see him win. Put the town on the map I reckon.'

Sally looks up, as Jerry canters past on Star Chaser.

'Where's Tommy Holt then?' Meeks says. 'Slept in?'

'Must have' Sally says.

'Bloody jockeys, lazy bastards' he says. 'Well good luck Sally, I hope she can do it for you.'

Sally raises her binoculars to find Jerry once more, his hands gently caressing the reins, as he starts to ease the mare down. Her rich, chestnut coat is shining in the dim morning light. Her father would be pleased.

CHAPTER 13

Sally makes the twenty minute journey to the Frankston Hospital, rehearsing in her mind, how best to relay the news to her father. The news that Tommy Holt, loyal Tommy, brave Tommy, Tommy the magnificent, has sacked Star Chaser to ride Lord Melbery.

The nursing staff should be on standby with the pain killers.

Sally takes the elevator to the second floor. She steps outside and walks along the corridor leading to her father's ward, just as she hears an almighty crash. A stainless steel tray has been hurled in the air, descending quickly to the floor.

A young nurse exits the ward and skips along the corridor, her uniform freshly decorated with egg yolk and splattered with baked beans.

She glances at Sally as they pass one another.

'Bad news' she says.

Jack Morgan grips a copy of the Herald Sun in his fist, thrusting it towards Sally as she enters the ward.

The back page headline reads;

HOLT SWITCHES TO CUP FAVOURITE.

'What the hell is this?!' he demands.

Sally shrugs her shoulders.

'When did you find out then?' he says.

'He rang last night' Sally says. 'Wanted to talk to you but I explained you were laid up in here.'

'What the hell...' Jack raises his voice and then lowers his tone, '...is he doing?'

Sally conveys the content of her conversation with Tommy Holt. How he suspected Albert Maressmo was responsible for Da Silva's death, the same jockey that pulled up Bridal Waltz in last year's Cup and that he felt obliged to ride Lord Melbery.

Jack folds his good arm across his chest and grits his teeth. 'I'll never put that bastard on again' he says.

They are both silent for a moment before Sally asks 'What do we do now Dad?'

'Get out of here for a start' he says. 'They wanted me to stay 'til tomorrow, but thank God, they're going to drop me back this afternoon. At least I can watch the races on the TV.'

'But who do we get to ride her?' Sally says.

Jack sighs. 'I don't know' he says. 'They'll all be on show today I suppose, but she's only got fifty one and a half and I don't want to put some bloke on who has to waste for days to make the weight. They're not going to be much good to us at the end of two miles if that's the case. And if this business with Maressmo is true, then who on earth do you trust? Bloody hell, if he's paying people to pull them up to win on the punt, what's he going to do when he owns the favourite?'

Sally picks up the newspaper and opens it from the back page. There is a story relating to the ongoing investigation into the death of Alan Da Silva and a full page pictorial tribute to the former jockey. Apparently the police have spoken with the race club stewards and arranged to interview various jockeys and trainers at today's meeting.

She turns to the centre pages and the lift out form guide.

Jack had decided some weeks ago, not to run Star Chaser on the Saturday before the Cup. The mare had a hard run on a soft track in the Caulfield Cup and would derive no benefit from racing again so close to the event. Lord Melbery is not engaged and neither are any of the overseas entries.

The form guide lists the latest bookmaker odds for Tuesday's Melbourne Cup. Lord Melbery is the favourite at four to one. The English horse Prince Akabah is quoted at six to one and Laughing Clowns, the Caulfield Cup winner, seven to one. Sally's eyes scan down the page, past the names of horses listed at ten, twelve and fourteen to one. Star Chaser is not among them. Yesterday the mare was rated a twelve to one chance, today she is quoted at odds of twenty five to one.

Sally tells her father that she is sure everything will work out and that she is looking forward to him getting back into the fray. She says goodbye, takes the stairs to the ground floor and returns home.

Parking her car at the top of the drive, she walks into the house, to find Jerry standing in the kitchen.

'John O'Connor rang Sally' he says.

'Thought he might' she says.

'Three times' Jerry says, 'and a couple of journalists too, but they said they would ring back'

'Okay thanks' she says. 'Is everything else alright?'

'Hundred per cent' Jerry says. 'All the horses ate up. Star Chaser licked her bin clean.'

'That's good to hear' Sally says, as she picks up the phone.

A telephone rings once in the hallway of John O'Connor's home.

'Hello' he says.

'Hello John, Sally Morgan.'

'Sally, what the hell is going on?' he says.

'Well he just jumped off her' she says.

'Why? She hasn't broken down has she?' he says.

'No she's absolutely fine' Sally says, 'He just got a better offer I guess.'

'A better offer?!' John protests. 'You've got to be kidding, he's ridden her every start this time in, and all her work for the past two weeks.'

'Well he didn't ride her this morning, Jerry did' Sally says.

'And she's okay, there's nothing wrong with her?' he asks.

'Never better' she says.

'I'm going to the races today' he says, 'I can try to speak to him.'

'I really wouldn't bother John' she says. 'He rang last night, just let it go.'

'Well what did he say?' he demands.

'Just that he had been offered the ride on Lord Melbery' she says 'and he wants to keep in with people like Lewis and Maressmo I guess.'

There is a moment's silence before John continues.

'How's your Dad doing anyway?' he asks.

'He's okay' Sally says. 'Coming home this afternoon, so we will be back to normal.'

'Well hardly normal, surely' he says.

'Well no, not really' Sally says.

'But who do we get to ride her?' he asks.

'Dad will think about it this afternoon and let you know. Anyway I've got to go. Good luck today' she says and hangs up the phone.

Chapter 14

A large crowd converges on the entrance to Flemington racecourse. With newspaper form guides and binoculars at the ready, the collective mass shuttles along the bitumen walkways, under a mass of pink and yellow roses, set amidst a row of green, metal arches. The Nursery and Birdcage car parks, play host to hundreds of smartly dressed picnickers, where small marquees and market umbrellas flank an array of European motor cars and four wheel drives.

John O'Connor makes his way to the member's entrance, reminding himself that his car is parked near the big gum tree on row J1.

'Just the one thanks' he says, handing a ten dollar note to a teenage race book seller, elevated to a height in excess of six feet, courtesy of a plastic milk crate.

The boy digs into the pocket of his apron, rummaging amongst a handful of coins, as a shining, white stretch limousine sleeks along the driveway and pulls up at the gate.

Some of the crowd stop to watch, as a uniformed driver, steps out. He walks briskly around to the side of the car, opens the door and stands to attention.

A grey and black, striped trouser leg emerges, planting a black leather shoe on the bitumen. It is soon followed by another. Next comes, a broad, left hand holding a grey top hat and sporting a gold watch on its wrist. Finally the totality of the figure emerges, hoists itself upright and places the top hat on its head.

The limousine passenger is a huge, dark man with thinning grey hair. He is wearing a traditional morning suit. Metres of fabric have been dedicated to the waistcoat alone. His face is large, round and sour. Projecting a surly frown, he appears to disapprove of all that surrounds him. His name is Albert Maressmo.

He glances across to see John O'Connor. The two racehorse owners briefly stare at each other before the boy hands O'Connor his change.

Maressmo waddles towards a gate at the right of the designated entrance, where he is welcomed by an attendant and ushered into the course. The gate is shut behind him as John O'Connor joins the queue at the turnstiles.

Inspector Frank Dennis is standing in the scales area behind the mounting yard, speaking with chief steward Jim Cutler.

'And they weigh in again after the race before we give the all clear' Cutler says

The Chief Steward is giving the Inspector a crash course in race day procedures, oblivious to the fact it is an entirely familiar process to the former jockey. He points to the scales used to weigh the riders, together with their saddles and allotted handicap weights.

Dennis indulges him politely and patiently, asking for the names of those jockeys closest to the late Alan Da Silva and writing them in a notebook.

'What are your own recollections?' Dennis says. 'Was he ever in trouble with the stewards?'

'Da Silva?' Cutler says.

'Yes' the Inspector confirms.

'Nothing out of the ordinary really' Cutler says. 'The occasional careless riding charge, but for the most part he was very professional. We were concerned to hear that he gambled quite a lot though.'

'Is that at the casino or on the horses?' Dennis asks.

'Well in truth, both' Cutler says.

'But jockeys aren't allowed to bet' Dennis says.

'No they're not' Cutler says. 'It's not something we encourage, but it's not something we police all that vigorously either to be honest.'

'Did he gamble large sums?' Dennis asks.

'Apparently' Cutler says, 'but we've never had reason to question his commitment with any of his rides. As I said he was a thorough professional.'

Dennis stands with his arms folded, as a door opens on the far side of the scales area. A sign on the door reads Jockeys' Room. A small man emerges wearing a bright red and yellow silk jacket. He is followed by another, equally colourful, in lime, blue and pink stripes.

A succession of jockeys leave the room and walk into the mounting yard, Dennis noting their initials and surnames printed on the side of their white riding pants. Referring to the names he has scribbled in pencil, he makes a series of notes.

Yellow with the red Maltese cross is Fred Watkins, lime, blue and pink is Keith Smith and blue with white sleeves Tommy Holt. Just some of the names the chief steward has given him.

Cutler excuses himself and leaves the Inspector alone to observe the pre race ritual. Dennis walks outside and stands under the shade of the overhanging grandstand.

The jockeys greet the trainers and are in turn introduced to their horse's owners. There is much shaking of hands, followed by earnest and detailed instruction. Much of which is accompanied by precise hand gestures from the trainers and nods of acknowledgment from the jockeys.

'Thank you riders mount up!' comes a cry from one of the stewards, as a tribe of colourfully dressed individuals wanders about the enclosure in search of their mounts.

Punters are crowded ten deep, looking over a wall of white, yellow and pink roses. Many look up to study the horses, referring back to their race books and form guides, making last minute assessments of their investment's condition.

The field is led onto the track, as the owners and trainers make their way to seats in the grandstand. Numerous stewards are despatched to various points of the course, as several punters beat a path to the betting ring.

John O'Connor has found a seat opposite a giant video screen on the inside of the track. As the field is loaded into the barriers for the first race, his eyes span the length of the straight. He imagines Star Chaser bursting clear and setting up an unassailable lead. His enthusiasm tempered by the fact that twenty three other owners are probably doing exactly the same thing and that unlike the horse he bred and races in partnership with Jack Morgan, twenty three other horses have a confirmed and committed rider.

Before long, the runners in the first race sweep into the straight, their riders urging them forward; some feeling the sting of the whip. As they race past John O'Connor, it is the horse with the blue and white colours that bursts clear. Tommy Holt looks over his shoulder to see his nearest rivals are two lengths adrift, as his mount cruises to a comfortable victory.

Inspector Frank Dennis stands on the balcony above the mounting yard as an elated group of owners return, hugging and kissing one another and slapping their successful trainer on the back.

He watches a smiling Tommy Holt return to scale, touching the brim of his cap with the handle of his whip.

The other jockeys return, dismount and explanations ensue, as to why it is not that horse's owners standing in the winner's enclosure laughing, clapping and rubbing their hands together.

The chief steward had suggested that immediately after each race would be the best time for the Inspector to speak with some of the jockeys. In particular he should target those who are not riding in the following race. Fred Watkins would be first.

Watkins leaves his saddle, whip and cap in the Jockeys'

Room and emerges to answer the Inspector's invitation for a chat. As he listens and speaks, he unbuttons his silks, unzipping a safety vest and gently fanning his chest.

A veteran in a young man's sport, Watkins is forty three and looks fifty. His face is lean, hungry and dark. His cheeks are hollow and creased, his chin prominent and scarred. Dennis can see the outline of the jockey's ribs and wonders if there is a single trace of fat on his bones.

Watkins tells him he was shocked to hear of Da Silva's death, that he was well liked, professional and gifted.

'What about his relationship with Albert Maressmo?' Dennis asks.

'What about it?' Watkins says.

'I understand they were quite close and that Da Silva had some sort of sponsorship arrangement with the casino' Dennis says.

'He was paid to ride track work wearing a Crown Casino jacket and cap that sort of thing. He probably had to attend a few press conferences too I suppose. Plenty of the boys are on a similar deal' Watkins says.

'And you're not?' Dennis says.

'Nah. Too old, too ugly' he says smiling.

Dennis nods his head and asks bluntly. 'Would Da Silva ever make sure that a horse he was riding got beaten in a race or take steps to...'

'Absolutely not' Watkins interrupts. 'Look, there are that many rumours flying around about the bloke pulling things up and falling foul of the wrong people. It is the greatest load of bull shit I've ever heard. There is enough money in this game if you're a hundred per cent honest anyway and no one would dare risk it.'

'Are you sure about that?' Dennis asks, reminding himself the chief steward had no illusions that Da Silva and other jockeys for that matter, were involved in illegal betting activities.

'Like I said' Watkins says 'Bull shit rumours.'

'Okay thanks' Dennis says, folding his notebook shut.

'Anytime' Watkins says, as he walks away.

Dennis steps down from the balcony and looks up at the sky, cutting a conspicuous figure and a small shadow, as he walks about the empty mounting yard.

Albert Maressmo watches him from the confines of his private box. The man in the grey suit wandering across the lawn, bears a striking resemblance to the 'rather dour Inspector fellow' that his PR manager had described to him.

The casino boss puffs on a large cigar, as the policeman refers to his notes.

CHAPTER 15

The door to Albert Maressmo's private box is held open as Frank Dennis steps inside.

'Welcome Inspector' Maressmo says smiling, extending his hand for the policeman to grip and shake.

An impressive array of food adorns tables draped in crisp while linen, all placed behind panels of glass that allow an uninterrupted view of the racecourse.

'Please, help yourself to some food' Maressmo says, adding 'May I offer you something to drink?'

'Thank you but no' Dennis says.

'Well then' Maressmo says, clasping his hands together. 'How can I help?'

'I wanted to speak to you about Alan Da Silva' Dennis says.

'Yes, of course' Maressmo says, 'ghastly business.'

'Ghastly indeed' Dennis says. 'Tell me Mr. Maressmo. I understand that your association with Alan Da Silva spanned several years.'

'Yes indeed Inspector' Maressmo says, 'Alan rode for me many times in the past and we enjoyed some tremendous success together.'

'What about away from the track?' Dennis asks.

'We were friends certainly' Maressmo says, 'good friends.'

'I understand he was a regular patron of the casino?' Dennis says.

'Yes he was' Maressmo confirms. 'In fact we had a sponsorship arrangement in place. One that has always worked to our mutual benefit I am sure.'

'And a substantial line of credit that allowed him to wager quite large sums and accumulate some very heavy losses' Dennis says.

'I am not sure I would describe it as substantial Inspector' Maressmo says. 'He was a man of quite generous means after all,' adding 'I certainly hope you are not suggesting that I or any of my associates were involved in this dreadful episode.'

'Well it did happen under your roof Mr. Maressmo and I must say the timing of it all is rather suspicious' Dennis says.

Maressmo protests, 'And just how I am supposed to have benefited? 'I have lost my jockey. I have lost my friend and I have suffered a personal and PR disaster as a consequence.'

Unperturbed, Dennis continues.

'When you say Da Silva rode for you?' he says, 'Do you mean to say he rode horses that you owned or that he rode others in a manner that allowed you to benefit?'

Maressmo fixes the policeman with an angry stare.

'I am a businessman Inspector. Not a criminal' he says.

Maressmo extends an arm and gestures towards the door.

'I think we're done here' he says.

'For now' Dennis replies.

CHAPTER 16

John O'Connor wanders through the betting ring as queues of winning punters form at the bookmaker stands and tote pavilions. The last race has been run and with the exception of the diehards investing on the final events interstate, the majority of race goers are either filling various bars or car parks. Some are sipping champagne on the lawn, while others are stuck in traffic.

O'Connor is one of twenty four people who have an appointment in the Committee Room. At 6.00pm the Victoria Racing Club will conduct the barrier draw for Tuesday's Melbourne Cup and each horse's owner or duly appointed representative, is required to randomly select a barrier for their horse. Jack Morgan had given him this responsibility some days before, together with the strict instructions 'draw something inside ten and give us a call straight away.' Nervous and excited he dreads making a phone call to say he has selected twenty four.

An open invitation exists for all owners to 'enjoy a drink with the committee' but John O'Connor prefers to wander on his own, repeating the affirmation 'anywhere inside ten.'

A roar echoes from the television monitors near the interstate bookmakers, as a handful of jubilant punters cheer home the favourite in Sydney. O'Connor reminds himself not to make quite so much noise if he manages to draw barrier one. Behaviour the committee would likely deem inappropriate, not to mention embarrassing in full view of the television cameras.

An outside barrier may not be a disaster by the same token. The field has a run of 900 metres to the first turn, with plenty of time to get a position close to the fence. Staying wide early could mean your horse avoids some of the interference that can occur early in the race, especially if the pace is modest. Even so, an inside gate will help, as Jack will want Star Chaser to position herself in the first half of the field at least. Thereafter her jockey, as yet unknown, will try to 'put her to sleep' for the bulk of the race. Two miles is further than the mare has raced before but this is the case for most of the runners and she had always given the impression she would handle the trip.

At ten minutes to six, O'Connor steps on to an escalator that transports him to the first floor of the grandstand. He takes a mobile phone from his pocket and checks Jack Morgan's number is stored in the menu.

A small, elderly man in a navy blue uniform checks his invitation at the door and ushers him inside. Should anyone decide to crash the event, the first wave of resistance will not hold for long.

Television crews are setting up cameras and tripods in front of a small stage, as a waitress presents O'Connor with a selection of drinks on a tray. He lightens her load by a glass of beer, curious that none of the bar staff in any other part of the racecourse are as young or as pretty.

A large backdrop stretches across the wall behind the stage. It is painted to resemble the starting stalls and as each horse is allocated a barrier, an official will hang an icon of a jockey wearing the relevant horse's colours in place. John O'Connor hopes to see a set of black and white stripes, yellow sleeves and cap, somewhere close to the door. Appropriately perhaps, the outside barrier is adjacent to the toilets.

Victoria Racing Club chairman Sir Donald Simpson steps up on stage and stands behind a lectern. He raises his hand to shield his eyes from the lights, reassures himself that his audience is still present, unfolds a page of notes and clears his throat.

He welcomes the successful owners and assembled media, as the imposing figure of Albert Maressmo enters the room, accompanied by a thick trail of cigar smoke. A grey top hat sits atop his head, perched at a precarious angle.

Momentarily distracted, the chairman explains that each horse's owner will be invited to select a miniature Melbourne Cup trophy from the twenty four laid out on a small table in front of the stage. A different number is printed on the base of each miniature, corresponding to one of the twenty four barriers in the race. Owners will be invited to select a barrier in saddlecloth number order. Whomever represents the English horse Prince Akabah will be first to choose.

A middle aged man with a pale complexion steps

forward. He leans over the table and lifts a miniature from the centre of the selection. He turns it upside down, looks at the base and in a cultured accent calls out 'Seventeen.' He looks about him not sure what to do and is invited to keep it. He smiles, remarks 'First of many I hope' puts the trophy in his jacket pocket and merges into the crowd. A royal blue jockey icon is attached to the backdrop in the number seventeen barrier position, as Albert Maressmo is invited to choose a barrier for Lord Melbery. Holding a cigar in his right hand he snatches a trophy with his left, barks 'thirteen' and lays the miniature on the edge of the table.

'Two down and none inside ten, then barrier five is drawn.

The process continues through horses eleven and twelve. O'Connor's eyes fix on the colourful display. Half the barriers have been drawn and six gates inside ten remain, as do the two on the extreme outside. Nineteen, fifteen, six and ten are allocated, before 'one' is claimed. An aqua and pink jockey icon is placed in position, amidst polite applause from the back of the room.

'Number eighteen, Town Hall' calls the chairman, as a middle aged woman in a hat the size of the stage, walks forward. 'Twenty three' she says quietly, but loud enough to spark a faint murmur in the audience.

'Number nineteen, Pride of Killarney' Sir Donald announces.

'Three' the horse's owner confirms.

'Damn' O'Connor whispers.

Five horses are left and barriers seven, twelve, sixteen, twenty and twenty four remain.

'Number twenty, Rochester' calls the chairman. A tall fair haired man walks forward and draws the barrier that corresponds to his horse's saddlecloth number. His head bows in disappointment.

Cheer up mate, could be worse, O'Connor mutters to himself, as the chairman calls 'Number twenty one, Star Chaser.'

John O'Connor walks towards the stage, squinting under the powerful lights. He looks at the remaining miniatures. Only four remain; barriers seven, twelve, sixteen and twenty four. He reaches across the table and picks up the one set furthest away, gripping it firmly in his fist. Anything but twenty four he thinks to himself, as he unclenches his fingers, turns it upside down and reads the number printed white against a black background and glued to a green felt base. He looks up to see that a jockey icon, sporting black and white stripes, yellow sleeves and white cap is being held in front of the backdrop, ready to be placed in position.

'Seven' he says.

Jack Morgan's colours fill the last remaining single digit barrier, as O'Connor walks to the side of the room. He takes his mobile phone from his pocket when he is interrupted.

'You would be happy with that then?' an unfamiliar voice offers.

'Well it's a start' O'Connor says, looking at the ID badge Inspector Frank Dennis is holding in front of him.

'Bit of a shock, Tommy Holt jumping off your horse' the Inspector says.

'Yeah, you could say that' O'Connor says.

Tell me' Dennis says, 'Did you ever meet Alan Da Silva?'

'I can't say that I did no' O'Connor says.

'He never rode your horse then?' Dennis asks.

'No never' O'Connor says.

'Still, his death hasn't done you any favours has it? I mean how do you get another jockey at this stage?' Dennis says.

'Well, there are plenty of jockeys Inspector, just not so many good ones' O'Connor says.

Dennis nods his head.

'Like a bet do you?' he asks.

'Now and then' O'Connor says.

'Casino?' Dennis asks

'Nah. Not my scene' O'Connor says.

'Really?' Dennis says. 'My understanding is you are a bit of a regular.'

'I wouldn't say that' O'Connor says.

'So you weren't there last Thursday night, Friday morning?' Dennis asks.

'No, I was at home. Probably asleep' O'Connor says.

'Can anyone verify that?' Dennis asks, 'Wife, girlfriend?'

'No I live alone' O'Connor says.

'What about Albert Maressmo?' Dennis asks 'ever met him?'

'No' O'Connor says.

Dennis looks O'Connor squarely in the eye.

'Okay' he says, 'best you make your phone call.'

'Thanks' O'Connor says, turning his back.

Sally Morgan answers his call.

'Hi Sally' he says, 'John O'Connor.'

'How did we go?' she asks anxiously.

'Seven' he says proudly.

'Seven' she relays to her audience.

Jerry punches the air, as Jack nods and smiles.

'Well done' she says.

'It was the best of what remained, we could have got twenty four' he says excitedly.

'That's great John' she says, 'Listen, Dad said to come down for lunch tomorrow. We should have a jockey booked by then.'

'Who is in the frame?' he asks.

'Tell you tomorrow' she says.

CHAPTER 17

It is Sunday morning when Frank Dennis parks his car outside a two storey red brick house in a quiet, leafy part of Armadale.

He strolls through an open wrought iron gate, steps onto a stone paved veranda and presses the doorbell.

An attractive woman in her mid thirties opens the door. She tosses a mane of long black hair over her shoulder, as the policeman presents her with his ID.

'Mrs. Da Silva' he says. 'Frank Dennis. We spoke on the phone earlier.'

'Yes, of course. Come in' she says, stepping back from the doorway and ushering him inside.

'Please come through' she adds, walking into a spacious lounge room where an older woman, dressed in black is sitting on a white leather couch.

'This is my mother' she says.

'Mum. This is Inspector Dennis. The man we spoke with on the phone.'

The older woman leans forward 'How do you do?' she says.

'Hello' Dennis says, as he is invited to sit down.

Da Silva's widow sits next to her mother, while Dennis perches on the edge of a chair.

'I am very grateful that you would agree to speak with me and I just want to say that I am very sorry for your loss. I am sure this is a very difficult time' he says.

Da Silva's wife nods and says 'yes' as her mother reaches into her lap to hold her hand.

'I don't suppose you can shed any light on what transpired last Friday morning?' he says.

Da Silva's widow shrugs her shoulders and shakes her head.

'Are you aware of any threats or difficulties that your husband may have encountered, any unsolicited phone calls, knocks at the door, that sort of thing' he asks.

'No, nothing like that' she says.

'What about his relationship with Albert Maressmo?' Dennis asks. 'Was that always cordial and above board?' he asks.

'Yes, I think so' she says. 'He did ask a lot of Alan all the same.'

'When you say, he asked a lot. What do you mean by that exactly?' Dennis says.

'Well, Alan was asked to make any number personal appearances. Photos with celebrities, that sort of thing and all the while he was expected to spend a lot of money at the casino.' she says.

'You mean wager or gamble a lot of money' Dennis says.

Da Silva's widow sighs, 'Albert was very good to us' she

says. 'He was always very generous but all the same, I think Alan probably gave back most of what he earned.'

'Losing money at the casino?' Dennis says.

'Yes' she says. 'I tried not to interfere, as Alan always said it was important to maintain a good relationship.'

'What about some of his fellow jockeys?' Dennis says, 'Were any of them particularly envious or angry towards him for any reason.'

'I don't think so' she says. 'I know he had a few altercations over the years, with one or two people, but it's a very competitive industry and there is a lot of money at stake' she says, adding 'Alan always said he had to make hay while the sun shone. You are a long time retired he would say.'

'Mrs. Da Silva I have to ask, where were you last Friday morning when your husband was killed?' Dennis says.

'I was in bed, fast asleep' she says sternly. 'That was until the phone rang.'

'So you didn't accompany your husband to the casino earlier that evening?' Dennis asks.

'No' she says, adding 'We finished dinner just after eight and Alan left shortly before nine I think.'

'We recovered your husband's mobile phone but he doesn't appear to have contacted you at any stage while he was at the casino' Dennis says.

'No he didn't' she says.

'Do you own a car Mrs. Da Silva?' Dennis asks.

'Yes, of course' she says.

'Perhaps I could see it?' Dennis asks.

Da Silva's widow stands up. She walks out of the lounge and leaves the house by the front door with the Inspector following.

She steps off the veranda, points a remote control unit and raises a garage door to reveal a late model white Audi.

Dennis steps inside the garage and slowly circles the vehicle, as Da Silva's widow folds her arms across her chest.

'It's not damaged Inspector' she says.

CHAPTER 18

John O'Connor parks his car at the top of the driveway next to the Morgan's modest weather board. He steps out and locks the door, as Sally swings the fly wire open, letting it slam shut behind her.

'Good idea to lock it!' she calls out, 'Lots of nefarious characters lurking around here!'

'Force of habit' he says.

'Hi, how are you?' Sally says smiling.

'Fine thanks,' he says 'very excited.'

'Come on, we'll have a look at her' Sally says, walking towards the stables.

John skips for a few strides to catch Sally, asking 'Is everything alright?'

Sally laughs. 'She's fine. Don't believe everything you read in the papers.'

The press have printed stories suggesting Tommy Holt switched to Lord Melbery because all is not well with Star Chaser. Apparently she has a bruised hoof and the stewards intend conducting a veterinary inspection, before she can take her place in the field.

'Not exactly the start to the day I was looking for I can tell you' he says.

'I suppose they have to write about something' Sally says 'Other than Da Silva at least.'

'I guess so' he says.

'Anyway we've got more important things to worry about' Sally says, flicking the latch and sliding open the door to Star Chaser's stable.

John steps inside and slides the door closed behind him, whispering nervously to Sally 'She looks great.'

Sally rubs the mare's neck, as Rosie nudges her head against her waist, nibbling at the buckle of her jeans.

O'Connor swallows hard and leans against the wall, his hands behind his back, watching on jealously, as his own horse plays and flirts with Sally in the very manner he longs to himself.

Sally retreats from the attention. She cups the mare's jaw in both hands and berates her for being 'a cheeky girl.'

'Well give her a pat' she says, 'she'll think you don't love her anymore.'

John steps forward, gently stroking his horse's neck.

'She's doing really well. We've just got to hope for some luck' Sally says. 'Anyway, come and have a chat to Dad.'

They both step outside, closing the door and fixing the latch.

The couple stroll towards the house, Sally tucking the tail of her shirt into her jeans, as John walks beside her.

She opens the door and kicks off her boots, as John O'Connor fumbles at the laces of his shoes.

'Leave them on if you want' she says.

'No its okay' he says, dragging them from his feet.

They walk into the lounge where Jack is sitting on the couch, beneath a row of photographs featuring many of Star Chaser's race wins.

'G'day mate' John says looking at Jack. 'How are you feeling?'

Jack shuffles in his chair, grimacing. 'I'll be right' he says.

'Have a seat' Sally says, as she sits down next to her father.

John sits down, as Sally points a remote control at the television, switching it off.

John O'Connor is excited. All he wants to talk about is Star Chaser and the Melbourne Cup. Who will ride her? What is the strategy? What will your instructions be? But he resists, politely enquiring 'So how long will you be laid up like this?'

Jack sighs 'About eight weeks they reckon' he says, 'then I have got a course of physio.'

'So where's the culprit then?' John asks.

'We shot him' Jack says dryly.

'Oh, actually, I meant Jerry' John says.

'So did I' Jack says, adding 'Nah, he's at home with his mum and dad.'

Sally looks at her father feigning disapproval, before assuring their guest 'And the horse is in his stable, alive and well in case you're wondering.'

'Sure. Let the boy spend a day with his family' Jack says. 'We can shoot him tomorrow' adding 'so, how did you go yesterday?'

'Well I drew a barrier' John says proudly, clenching his fist in triumph.

'You did indeed' Jack confirms.

John produces the miniature Melbourne Cup trophy he had selected the night before and tells Jack and Sally about his barrier draw experience. He waxes lyrical about the lights of the television cameras, the colourful barrier stalls and jockey icons, to say nothing of the swarming journalists.

'Oh the press' Jack says, 'they won't leave us alone. We've taken the phone of the hook. Between them and all the jockey managers and agents it hasn't stopped.'

'But you've booked someone to ride her?' John says.

'Yep' Jack says.

'Who?' he asks.

I've booked a New Zealand jockey' Jack says. 'Colin Shearer.'

John thinks for a moment and says 'He won the Flight Stakes in Sydney on Apple Sauce.'

'That's the one' Jack says.

'He rode a horse in the straight race yesterday, one of Hartford's, Message Sent' John says.

'That's him' Jack says. 'He's come over just for the carnival. Mainly to ride that filly in the Oaks but I like him. He's got a good record in big races and he rides on a long rein. I reckon he will suit her. She'll need to settle if she's going to have a sprint left at the end of two miles.'

'Can he make the weight alright? That thing he rode yesterday had about fifty seven kilos' John says.

'Well he's listed in the calendar at fifty one and he assures me that he's around fifty two and a half now, so he's just got to watch himself for a couple of days and we should be right' Jack says.

'That's terrific Jack. I'm sure he will do a great job' John says.

'Well he's coming down in the morning to get the feel of her. Just to trot her around the place and he seems a decent enough bloke.'

Jack and Sally sit down to lunch with John, the conversation not straying from Tuesday's Melbourne Cup. Every aspect of the race is dissected and discussed in minute detail. Hours tick by as past glories are recalled and dreams are ventured.

Just as they finish lunch, a key slides into the lock of room 207 at the Carlton Crest Hotel. A short, dark haired man enters, tossing a sweat stained towel on the floor. A two hour gym work out has left him exhausted, dehydrated and dripping perspiration. He sits on the edge of a king size bed, peels a soaking tee shirt from his chest and drags a pair of running shoes and socks from his feet. He stands up, removing his shorts and underpants, his naked body reflected in the television, where three rows of type appear on the screen.

GOOD AFTERNOON

MR. C. SHEARER

ENJOY YOUR STAY

He walks into the bathroom, steps onto a set of scales, takes a deep breath and looks down.

54.7 kilograms.

'Shit' he says.

CHAPTER 19

Former bookmaker James Henderson sits alone in a modest St. Kilda cafe. He sips coffee from a cup, as Inspector Frank Dennis approaches and shakes his hand.

'Thank you for speaking with me' Dennis says.

'No problem' Henderson says, as the policeman sits down at his table.

'How's the real estate world?' Dennis asks.

'Oh, it has its moments' Henderson says.

James Henderson was once one of Melbourne's biggest and most successful bookmakers. He quickly rose through the ranks attracting a glamorous and well heeled clientele. He was handsome, confident and ruined when Albert Maressmo orchestrated a massive betting plunge on the previous year's Melbourne Cup.

Henderson's mistake was not dispersing some of Maressmo's outlay. Even backing Break of Day at a lesser price with other bookies would have reduced his exposure.

Instead he took every bet he could and stood the horse to lose a fortune. He gambled heavily and lost.

'You wouldn't think even Albert Maressmo could stitch

up an entire Melbourne Cup field' Henderson says.

'So you maintain the race was a fix' Dennis says.

'Of course it was!' Henderson says. 'You only need to look at the replay to see that. Everyone knew. But no one would dare say or do anything about it!'

'Not even the stewards?' Dennis asks.

Henderson laughs 'Least of all the stewards' he says.

'So what part do you believe Alan Da Silva played' Dennis asks.

'He was certainly in on it' Henderson says. 'They all were. Look at the replay if you don't believe me. Break of Day gets a cosy run for the whole trip and as soon as they turn for home, the leaders veer off the track, taking half the field with them. Break of Day gets a dream run, kicks clear and nothing, nothing gets out and runs on until it's all too late. It was an absolute boat race and nobody said, wrote or did anything.'

'And why do think that is?' Dennis asks.

'Because people have families Inspector' Henderson says sternly. 'They have families, children and livelihoods.'

Henderson swallows the last of his coffee, stands up and walks out.

CHAPTER 20

6.20 am Monday and Jack, Sally and Jerry are waiting for Colin Shearer, the man who will pilot Star Chaser in tomorrow's Melbourne Cup. Assuming she passes a rumour driven veterinary inspection.

Jack shuffles his feet impatiently, while Sally and Jerry stand with arms folded, looking at the ground. Their reserves of polite conversation exhausted, the trio stand quietly, as a diminutive figure walks briskly towards them.

'Jack!' he calls out. 'Colin Shearer. Sorry I'm late. I didn't realise how far it was.'

Jack had asked his new rider to be at the track no later than 5.30 am and to allow an hour to drive from Melbourne. Surely a Melbourne Cup ride was incentive enough to get up early.

'Righto' Jack replies, not disguising the fact he is unimpressed with the jockey's tardiness.

'What happened to you anyway?' Shearer asks.

'You should see the other bloke' Jack says dryly, introducing Sally as his daughter and Jerry as Jerry.

'Colin Shearer' the jockey says, shaking Sally's hand and

'How are ya' as he greets Jerry.

Sally folds a cotton towel over the mare's back and lifts a saddle from the stable divide.

'I've got hold of most of her runs on video Jack' Shearer says, as Sally and Jerry fasten the saddle in place. 'Looks like she stays alright and she's got a good turn of foot.'

'Might have won a Caulfield Cup if the track wasn't wet' Jack says.

'So what's the plan this morning?' Shearer asks.

'I don't want her to do anything much, just trot one lap and gently canter over a thousand metres. It's just for you to get a feel of her really.'

Shearer reaches up and rubs the mare's forehead. 'Are you going to look after me tomorrow girl?'

'She's pretty relaxed' Sally says. 'Not much bothers her.'

'Well I hope we can give them some bother eh' he says, as Jack hoists him into the saddle.

Sally leads both horse and rider towards the track, as Jack and Jerry follow.

It is well past six o'clock and already light. As a result, there is more activity both on and off the course.

Jack would expect to be home by now but instead he is accepting the well wishes of a handful of colleagues.

'Good luck Lefty!' someone calls out, as he walks by. Jack looks straight ahead, raising his one free hand in acknowledgement.

Colin Shearer holds the mare up at the entrance to the track, assessing the flow of traffic before asking her to trot a warm up lap. Jack leans over the rail, thinking there is nothing more he can do. His charge has never been fitter. She will go into the race fresh and with a good barrier. The rest, soon enough, will be up to C. Shearer.

Shearer's alarm had woken him at four am. Plenty of time to get dressed and make the one hour drive to Mornington well before 5.30am. Instead he took an elevator to the first floor, where he spent the best part of an hour skipping, cycling and punching a speedball. Three cigarettes constituted breakfast. Lunch will be a grapefruit and dinner a small bowl of brown rice. Each subsequent meal will be followed by a lap jogging around Albert Park Lake, a stint in the gym and half an hour in the sauna. He is well aware that Star Chaser is handicapped to carry fifty one and a half kilograms in the Melbourne Cup and that he has told Jack Morgan he will have no trouble making the weight. The stewards will allow him to ride half a kilo over, which means with one and a half kilos of saddle, safety vest and gear, he will need to weigh no more than fifty and a half kilograms by 3.00pm tomorrow.

The equation is simple, if the execution torturous. He must shed 4.2 kilograms in forty hours.

A leisurely track work session completed, Shearer trots the mare back to where Jack, Sally and Jerry are waiting.

Star Chaser breathes deeply and evenly, as her rider flicks his toes out of the stirrups and dangles his legs by her sides.

'I know we didn't do much but she moves beautifully Jack' the jockey says, adding 'she feels really strong and very clean winded.'

Jack explains that he wants the mare ridden up on the

pace, to make use of her barrier and be running in the first half of the field approaching the post the first time. That way if anyone is caught wide and forced to go forward she won't get shuffled too far back in the field. The key, he says, will be to get her to relax, to let her 'go to sleep' for the bulk of the two miles.

Shearer listens closely, as he slides the saddle from the mare's back.

Jerry hangs on every word, hoping one day that he too might receive a similar set of instructions.

'If you can get clear four hundred out, just go for home' Jack says, making a fist and thrusting his arm forward. 'She's only got fifty one and a half, so let them try and catch you. We've got the pull in the weights' he says excitedly.

Jack can sense a dulling of his jockey's enthusiasm.

'You with me?' he says, looking Shearer squarely in the eye.

'All the way Jack' Shearer says.

'How's your weight?' Jack says.

Shearer laughs. 'No worries there.'

'What do you weigh now then?' Jack says.

'About fifty two' Shearer says, 'but a stint in the sauna in the morning will see me right.'

'Have you got any other rides tomorrow?' Jack says.

'Just the one' Shearer confirms. 'I'm riding one Peter Bishop brought across in the 1400 metre race.'

'The race after the Cup?' Jack says.

'That's the one' Shearer says

'Nothing before?' Jack asks.

'Not at this stage' Shearer says.

It is of no great concern to Jack that Colin Shearer has not picked up many other rides. He is one of New Zealand's best jockeys and primarily in Melbourne to ride Apple Sauce in the Oaks on Thursday. Any other rides he might pick up along the way are a bonus, as most of the local trainers will employ their regular riders.

'So where are you staying anyway?' Jack asks.

'Carlton Crest' Shearer says.

'Stay out the restaurant' Jack says.

Shearer chuckles, 'I wouldn't know where it is' he says.

CHAPTER 21

Most of the fifteen hundred people crowded into the Galaxy Room at Crown Casino, have devoured their smoked salmon entrée before Inspector Frank Dennis arrives.

The traditional Call of the Card has attracted a veritable who's who of the racing industry to the Cup Eve lunchtime event, together with the sombre, street wise policeman who observes proceedings from the back of the room.

Waiting staff clear plates from tables, as a presenter walks on stage and stands behind a silver lectern with a metallic blue, Crown Casino logo. He glances to his right to see four men join him on stage.

The four sit behind a rectangular table, covered with the ever present casino branding.

Albert Maressmo and guests sit directly in front of the stage.

The presenter introduces the four men as 'our bookmakers Graham Bishop, Phillip Long, Ron Cartwright and Charlie Nettlefold.'

He explains that members of the audience will have the opportunity to place a bet on the horses running in tomorrow's

Melbourne Cup, with any of the four, at the odds each will quote. The bookmakers will take turns to quote each horse's price and all transactions will be conducted on a strict cash basis, unless prior arrangement has been made.

The rules and procedures are conveyed to the audience, as a waitress approaches a man standing at the back of the room.

'Can I help you find a seat sir?' she says.

'No thanks' Dennis says, his eyes focussed on the stage.

'It's just that it's a bit awkward with you here when we bring out the meals' she says, pointing to the kitchen doors to the Inspector's right.

'I'll stand over there then' he says nodding.

'Are you booked as part of a table?' she asks.

'No' he says, walking towards a palm tree in the corner of the room.

'Camouflage' he mutters to himself.

The room lights dim, as a highlight video is projected onto a large screen behind the stage. It shows the Melbourne Cup top weight Prince Akabah winning his last start at York in the UK.

The room lights come up, as the video ends and the presenter invites Graham Bishop to quote a price.

Bishop looks more like a stockbroker, than a bookmaker. He is in his mid-forties, tall and thin with neatly combed hair and glasses.

'Prince Akabah eight to one.'

'Eight to one Prince Akabah' the presenter repeats enthusiastically, asking 'if any of the other gentlemen care to offer a longer price.'

The three others shake their heads and members of the audience are invited to invest.

A show of hands alerts a team of tall, attractive females to relay microphones to punters in the audience.

The first bet is $8,000 to $1,000, followed by $4,000 to $500, and a succession of minimum $100 wagers.

The next horse to be offered is number twenty four, Golden Palace. He is not considered worthy of a video replay, before Phillip Long offers odds of one hundred to one and is claimed for a single bet of $10,000 to $100 from the horse's owner.

The room lights dim again, as a replay of the W. S. Cox Plate is introduced. The audience watches quietly as the late Alan Da Silva guides Lord Melbery to victory. The presenter bows his head, asking everyone 'to observe a minute's silence in memory of a great sportsman.'

The room falls quiet, with the exception of a few pots clattering in the kitchen. A photograph of the late jockey appears on the screen above the words Alan Da Silva 1978 – 2019, as a wisp of cigar smoke wafts in front of the stage.

'Thank you ladies and gentlemen' the presenter says. 'Ron Cartwright are you prepared to offer odds on Lord Melbery.'

The bookie shuffles forward in his seat, clears his throat, looks up and says 'Four to one Lord Melbery.'

All eyes turn to the man attached to the large cigar in front of the stage. Albert Maressmo is wearing a navy blue suit and a morbid expression. Lord Melbery's trainer, Len Lewis, is seated to his right. To his left is Tommy Holt and next to him, Tiffany Kirk-Jones.

Dennis cannot see the casino boss from the back of the room. A tall brunette, wearing Maressmo's racing colours of black jacket and red cap is standing in the way, holding a microphone.

Maressmo stands and buttons his jacket.

Conscious of the theatre he is generating and relishing his moment in the spotlight, Maressmo speaks slowly and deliberately. His words amplified around the room.

'I'll have four million to a million' he says.

His wager achieves its initial aim. A loud murmur spreads like a wave across the audience.

Ron Cartwright appears unmoved. 'You can have a million to two fifty Mr. Maressmo' he says.

There is a hum of disappointment in the room. Maressmo stays on his feet, as the presenter interjects. 'Charlie Nettlefold, are you prepared to offer four to one?'

The eldest of the quartet nods his head. 'Yes you can have a million to two fifty with me.'

Graham Bishop leans back in his chair. 'Yeah alright!' he calls out confidently.

'That's a million to two hundred and fifty thousand with you' the presenter confirms.

'Yep' he says.

Before he is invited to do so, Phillip Long speaks up 'Same here. You're on.'

'A million to two fifty with you Phillip' is confirmed from the lectern.

'Can I ask gentlemen, what price Lord Melbery now?' the

presenter says, looking to see that Maressmo still has hold of the microphone.

'Three to one' Ron Cartwright replies. His colleagues confirm their agreement.

Maressmo raises his arm, moving it from side to side, pointing a finger at each of the four bookmakers. 'Six hundred thousand to two hundred thousand with each one of you' he barks, handing the microphone back to the tall brunette.

The four bookmakers who walked on stage looking like investment bankers, now resemble a row of ducks in a shooting gallery.

They each make written notes, as Maressmo sits down.

Inspector Dennis walks into the foyer and makes a call on his mobile phone, returning to hear bookmaker Phillip Long offer odds of twenty to one for Star Chaser to win the Melbourne Cup. The mare is the medium of modest support, with a bet of $10,000 to $500 each way coming from a table in the centre of the room.

* * * * * *

John O'Connor sits alone on the couch in his lounge room. Credit card statements litter his coffee table - a legacy of his ill fated gambling endeavours and the motivation behind the restraining order his ex-wife and child had secured the previous year, lest his anger and frustration boil over again.

He stares remorsefully at a framed photo of his son, as the television recounts Star Chaser's various race victories - seven in all.

As the mare's career unfolds on the screen, he bows his head, praying for the sort of redemption a Melbourne Cup victory might bring.

He turns the volume up, as the mare races away with the Turnbull Stakes, Tommy Holt riding hands and heels to the line. Yet tomorrow it is Colin Shearer who will be in the saddle.

Shearer boasts an enviable record - twenty seven group one victories, both in Australia and New Zealand; over a thousand winners, including several in Hong Kong. He is talented, successful and at that same moment, jogging around Albert Park Lake wearing a heavy waterproof jacket, in a desperate bid to shed enough weight to take the ride.

CHAPTER 22

7.00am Melbourne Cup Day.

Colin Shearer has spent the last hour in the hotel gym. His leg muscles ache and threaten to cramp as he steps out of the shower.

He towels himself off and steps onto a set of scales. The display fluctuates between fifty and fifty five kilos, its range decreasing with each swing.

52 kilograms.

He wraps a towel around his waist and breaks two diuretic tablets from their foil casing, tossing them towards the back of his mouth. A tiny sip of water washes them down his throat.

Colin Shearer hopes to urinate two kilograms in the next eight hours.

He walks into his hotel suite, snatching a packet of cigarettes from the bedside table, when there is a knock at the door.

He opens it to see a copy of the Herald Sun lying at his feet.

The headline reads;

CUP BETTING PLUNGE

'Bookmakers are reeling from a spectacular betting plunge on pre-race favourite Lord Melbery at yesterday's Call of the Card'

'Lord Melbery's owner Albert Maressmo, stands to win $6.4 million from four bookmakers alone, if his horse can win today's Melbourne Cup.'

'Flippin' heck' he mutters to himself, when there is another knock.

He opens the door again to find Fred Watkins carrying a leather briefcase.

'Hello Colin' he says.

Shearer glances at the briefcase and steps away from the door.

Watkins enters the room and the two men sit down.

'I've got a proposition for you' Watkins says.

'Which is?' Shearer says.

'Conveyed by' Watkins glances at the newspaper, 'my supporters.'

'Your' Shearer mimics his pause, 'supporters.'

Watkins doesn't respond.

'Well, what is it then?' Shearer asks.

Watkins opens the briefcase and presents it to Shearer. It is filled to the brim with $100 notes.

'A hundred large Bill, cash' he says.

Shearer looks Watkins in the eye.

'I'll cop as much if I win' he says.

'Yeah, but you don't want to win' Watkins says.

'Is that supposed to be a threat?' Shearer says.

'Hey, don't shoot me' Watkins says, 'I'm just the messenger.'

'Oh great' Shearer says, 'so I am the one that gets shot then, or run over.'

'Look, I don't know anything about that' Watkins says. 'For all I know it was just some disgruntled punter.'

'That's a fair grudge' Shearer says.

'Maybe' Watkins says, 'but nothing to do with us.'

'Us?' Shearer says.

'Yeah, well believe me' Watkins says, 'that whole business hasn't done us any favours.'

Shearer quips 'There's that word again.'

'Look mate' Watkins says, 'you're only in town for a few days, my advice is just play the game, take the money and get on a plane.'

Shearer shakes his head and sighs.

'I should have stayed at home' he says.

* * * * * *

Jack Morgan has given his horses the morning off and afforded himself the luxury of sleeping in. It is 7.00am before he climbs out of bed. He walks into the kitchen, as Sally and Jerry return from a trip to the store to buy the paper and for Jerry's parents to wish them luck.

Sally tells her father about the massive betting plunge on Lord Melbery. How Albert Maressmo stands to win $6.4 million in addition to the $5 million in prize money.

'At least the bookies will be cheering for us' he says.

'Them and most of the town I reckon' Sally says proudly,

producing a giant 'Good Luck' card signed by hundreds of people who had visited the Chapman's corner store.

Jack scans the mass of names, some of which he doesn't even recognise.

'Well, she had better not disgrace herself' he says, handing the card to Sally.

'Come on then lad' he beckons to Jerry, 'give us a hand to check the truck.'

Jerry races ahead and tilts the cab on the Bedford, as Jack shuffles across the driveway. He peers at the engine and checks the oil, hoping its precious cargo will reach Flemington safely and on time.

A trip to Flemington would normally take just over an hour, but Cup Day will be different - a lot different. On a fine day the Melbourne Cup can be expected to attract a crowd in excess of 100,000 and all indications and forecasts are for just that. The weather bureau predicts the day to be fine and mild, with an expected top temperature of twenty seven degrees.

There is no way to beat the traffic, no short cuts and no express lanes for floats carrying Cup runners. Race goers will be arriving at the track already and the traffic along Racecourse, Epsom and Smithfield Roads will be heavy and slow moving.

With her father out of action, Sally will drive. Jack will sit in the cabin and Jerry in the back with the mare.

Jack enjoys a breakfast of toast and coffee before Sally helps to wrap his bandages and dressings in plastic bags, escorting him into the shower.

A lot of women will attend the Melbourne Cup in all manner of elaborate outfits, in an attempt to attract the attention of their peers, their rivals and if they're really lucky, various newspaper and magazine photographers. Sally Morgan will not follow suit. Hers will be an entirely practical outfit. Brown leather boots, moleskin jeans, cotton shirt and Akubra hat.

Jack steps out of the shower, rips off his plastic and pulls on the navy blue trousers of his only suit.

'Can you give us a hand darl?' he says.

Sally arrives on the scene, as her father struggles to fit his free arm through the sleeve of a shirt.

'You'll have to wear a tie you know' she says. 'They won't let you in otherwise.'

CHAPTER 23

Two hours and ten minutes pass before Sally turns the Bedford left off Epsom Road and through the entrance to Flemington Racecourse reserved for the exclusive use of trainers, jockeys and floats.

A cricket match has been in progress in the park on the other side of the road. Sally and Jack have seen three overs bowled and the score advance by eleven runs without loss, while the truck crept the last fifty metres to the driveway at the top of the hill overlooking the racecourse.

Rarely out of first gear for much of the past hour, the truck rolls freely down the winding tarmac in second and third.

Jerry had confirmed throughout the journey that the mare was coping well and that she appeared relaxed and comfortable.

Sally parks the truck behind the Birdcage entrance, between two large commercial floats. Jack opens the door and hops down from the cabin, relishing the opportunity to stretch his legs and feel the sun on his face.

He walks to the back of the truck and lowers the tail.

'You right there lad?' he says.

'No worries' Jerry replies, stepping onto the tail gate and handing a lead rope to Sally.

Sally leads the mare towards the horse entrance, while Jerry waits for Mr. Morgan.

'Star Chaser, race seven' Sally says to an official.

'I know who she is' the official replies enthusiastically. 'I've got her in my doubles!'

'Really?' Sally says. 'Well good luck!'

'Good luck to you' he says, looking at a list of names on a clipboard. 'Stall 115.'

Jack and Jerry make their way towards the stall, while Sally leads the mare around the Birdcage enclosure.

Flemington is playing host to a huge crowd. It is a little after midday and Sally looks up at the packed grandstands and a sea of colour on the lawns. People are moving in all directions. The well dressed to and fro from catered picnics and corporate events in the Member's Car Park, while the various take away food and alcohol caravans do a roaring trade.

'Hi Sally' says a voice from behind a small hedge.

Sally maintains a brisk pace, calling over her shoulder 'Hello John, got to keep moving.'

John O'Connor nods, enduring the attention of numerous punters, wondering which horse it is the attractive blonde is leading.

Sally completes another circuit.

'How are you?' she says cheerfully.

'Nervous' he says.

'You're not alone' she says.

Another circuit completed and Sally points to a row of Cypress trees.

'Dad's over there' she says.

'Yes I know' John says, edging past the crowd that has gathered three deep, virtue of the fact most of the runners in race three are paraded before them.

The appropriate owner's pass secures John O'Connor entry to the stalls where he sees Jack Morgan, standing with Jerry and another man he does not recognise.

'Hi Jack' he says excitedly, nodding hello to Jerry and the man in the grey suit.

'Hello John' Jack says, introducing the third man as 'Paul McAllister - chief vet with the stewards.'

'Oh okay' O'Connor says nervously, shaking the vet's hand.

'We are probably right now Jack' the vet says.

Confused, John looks at Jerry.

'Veterinary inspection' he says.

'Oh right' John says.

'The boss says it's nothing to worry about' Jerry says. 'Reckons she's never been lame a day in her life.'

'God, I hope not' John says.

Sally leads the mare onto the grass in the centre of the enclosure, as the vet crouches down, running his hand down all four of her limbs in turn. Pinching and gripping her tendons and bone, he picks up her feet, tapping the frog of each hoof with a small hammer.

Sally watches on with concern and suspicion. Tommy

Holt had said Albert Maressmo would stop at nothing to engineer a victory in the race. And that was before he had backed his own horse to win millions. Was this inspection motivated by something other than newspaper rumours?

She leads the mare away. The vet watches closely, as Sally trots her back and stands staring at the man who holds their fate in his hands. If Star Chaser should fail this test, there will be no avenue of appeal. Their race will be lost before it has begun.

The vet steps forward, his arms folded across his chest. He looks down, staring at the mare's feet. He sighs and looks across at an anxious Jack Morgan.

'She's fine' he says. 'Good luck.'

CHAPTER 24

Colin Shearer sits on the lowest of three cedar benches, in the sauna attached to the Jockeys' Room.

Outside, over a hundred thousand people are gathered in a mild twenty six degrees, enjoying a diet of champagne and beer.

Shearer sits with his head bowed, a towel wrapped around his waist. Beads of sweat trickle from his forehead and run down his nose. Diving to the floor, they mark their landing spots with dark misshapen circles.

A clock on the wall ticks over to 1.00pm. It was shortly after midday when the jockey scraped the first flow of perspiration from his chest and arms.

His session completed Shearer stands, opens the door and steps outside.

The door to the sauna does not close behind him before all the energy and consciousness drains from his head and body. He makes a feeble attempt to reach for the handle, before his body collapses in a clumsy heap.

Colin Shearer lies passed out on the floor of the Jockeys' Room, his legs bent, arms outstretched and head tilted back.

At 3.00pm he is due to ride Star Chaser in the Melbourne Cup. Less than two hours before the race he lies motionless, his eyes closed shut and mouth wide open.

* * * * * *

Jack Morgan paces nervously, while Sally and Jerry stand in the shade, either side of the mare. John O'Connor has been despatched for soft drinks.

'You should sit down Dad' Sally says, concerned that her father, like a nervous horse in the mounting yard, might use up all his energy before the race.

'I'm alright' he says, wiping his brow with his sleeve.

Jack had paid no attention to the various announcements made over the public address system detailing weight and gear changes for the forthcoming race, but the page bearing his own name stops him in his tracks.

'Would trainer Jack Morgan, trainer Jack Morgan, please report to the scales area immediately!'

Sally looks at her father. He looks at her and Jerry looks at them both.

'What is it Dad?' Sally says, her voice stuttered with concern.

'I dunno' he says.

Concerned, Sally asks 'Do you want me to come with you?'

'No it's alright' he says. 'You stay here. I won't be long.'

Jack makes slow but steady progress, walking side on to protect his injured shoulder, as he cuts a swathe through the biggest Cup Day crowd in fifty years.

Once inside the members' enclosure he makes better time, walking in front of the grandstand, where dozens of women parade on the lawn, underneath hats the size of small marquees, adorned with all manner of flowers and feathers.

He reaches the mounting yard just as the jockeys are asked to 'mount up' for race three and walks into the scales area, where chief steward Jim Cutler takes him aside.

'Thanks for coming by Jack. I need a word' he says.

Cutler directs him to the Stewards' Room, where they both sit down.

'I'm afraid we've got a problem' Cutler says. 'Colin Shearer has been taken to hospital. He collapsed a few minutes ago outside the sauna. The doctor says he's horribly dehydrated and needless to say totally out of commission, for today at least.'

Jack slumps in his chair, he bows his head and shakes it.

Cutler continues.

'Now the issue is this. Of all the jockeys engaged here today that can ride at fifty one and a half, all of them are committed to rides in the race. Now the rules simply don't allow us to let anyone ride more than half a kilo over, so unless we can find someone who can ride at fifty two, I'm afraid we are going to have to scratch her. There is of course a meeting at Wangaratta today and we could put a call through there to see if someone is available. But we can't allow anyone to forgo any existing rides and then there's the issue of getting them down here. I'm not even sure if a helicopter would make it in time. Assuming we can get one. I'm very sorry Jack, it's terrible luck I know.'

Jack's shoulder throbs violently, as he tries to collect his thoughts.

There is a knock at the door.

'Bear with me for a few minutes Jack' Cutler says, 'I have to watch this race.'

Several minutes pass before the scales area is once again a hive of activity. The jockeys engaged in the previous race return and weigh in under the chief steward's watchful eye, before he announces 'All clear.'

Jack listens to the proceedings, before the door opens again.

'What do we do Jack?' Cutler asks.

'Can one of your people fetch someone for me?' he says.

'Yes of course' Cutler says.

'Stall 115' Jack says. 'There's a young fellow there. Jerry Chapman. Ask him to come up here.'

Cutler opens the door.

'David! Can you do something for me?' he says.

A young man in a uniformed blazer, steps forward and receives a set of instructions from the chief steward.

'He's young and fit' Cutler says. 'He'll find him alright. What's the plan?'

'The boy's apprenticed to me' Jack says. 'He can ride her.'

'What's his name again?' Cutler says.

'Jerry Chapman' Jack confirms.

'He's a three kilo boy isn't he?' Cutler says.

'He is' Jack says.

'Well strictly speaking Jack, we aren't supposed to allow an apprentice to replace a senior rider, particularly in a Group One race, but as no one else appears to be available…'

Jack interrupts 'He can sit on alright.'

Resting his hand on his shoulder, he mutters to himself 'most of the time.'

'And he can make the weight?' Cutler says.

'No problem there' Jack says.

'Of course he can't use his claim' Cutler says.

'I am well aware of that' Jack says. 'What about Shearer's gear? Is that still about? He can borrow that.'

Cutler stands up and walks towards the door. 'I'll have someone check for you' he says.

CHAPTER 25

The door to the Steward's Room swings open and a bewildered Jerry Chapman is ushered inside.

Mr. Morgan is sitting at the corner of a long timber table.

'Have a seat son' he says.

The apprentice pulls a chair away from the table and sits down. He is nervous and worried he has done something wrong.

'Right' Jack says. 'Here's the situation.'

Jerry starts to breathe more easily, relieved to learn that there is a 'situation.'

Mr. Morgan continues.

'Colin Shearer is out of commission' Jack says. 'In fact he is in hospital.'

Jerry stares wide eyed at his master, not yet appreciating the significance of their unscheduled meeting.

'Apparently he was wasting like mad to make the weight and he's completely buggered himself up in the process' Jack says. 'In any case though, I want you to ride the horse.'

Jerry's expression doesn't change. So much so, Jack thinks perhaps the boy hasn't heard him.

He looks his apprentice in the eye.

'Jerry' he says, 'I want you to ride Star Chaser in the Melbourne Cup.'

Jerry stares at Mr. Morgan.

Mr. Morgan stares back.

'Today' Jack says.

Jerry's lips softly mouth the word 'Me?'

'I don't see any other jockeys in the room' Jack says. 'Do you?'

'No' Jerry says.

'Well. What do you think?' Jack says.

Jerry nods, swallows and says 'Good to go.'

* * * * * *

Fred Chapman is closing his store early. As he bolts the front door a large saucepan crashes to the floor upstairs.

His wife bursts into the lounge and stands bracing herself against the back of a chair, as the race day telecast confirms an important late riding change in the Melbourne Cup.

"Jockey Colin Shearer has been replaced aboard Star Chaser, by the apprentice rider Jerry Chapman."

'Fred!' she cries in the general direction of the stairway.

'Fred!!' she screams.

'What?!' he shouts back.

'Jerry's…!'

Unable to decipher his wife's message, Fred assumes some cruel and dreadful fate has somehow befallen their son.

He tackles the stairs two at a time and short of breath, finds his wife standing in the lounge.

'What is it?' he says, having reached the first floor in record time.

His wife grabs both his arms. She looks him in the eye and tightens her grip - painfully.

'Jerry's riding the horse!' she says.

'What horse?' Fred says.

Beryl Chapman loosens her grip and pushes her husband away.

'Oh for God's sake, he's riding Star Chaser in the Melbourne Cup!' she says.

'What are you talking about?' Fred says. 'They've got that New Zealand jockey'.

'No!' his wife demands, pointing at the television. 'He's not riding her. Jerry is!'

Fred utters the word 'Rubbish' just as the television confirms the news.

'Oh my God' he says, 'the Melbourne Cup.'

* * * * * *

'They're betting thirty three to one now' John complains to Sally. 'She was sixteens when we got here. I snapped up the only bloke betting twenty to one and that didn't last long.'

'I guess they're worried about the jockey' she says.

'Why? What's wrong with him all of a sudden?' John says.

'You didn't hear the announcement then?' Sally says.

'What? Have we declared war on New Zealand?' he says.

Sally shakes her head.

'Colin Shearer's not riding her' she says reluctantly. 'He

is, as they say, indisposed.'

'Oh shit! What happened?' John demands.

'I don't know' Sally says shrugging her shoulders.

O'Connor shuffles his feet and stutters his words. 'Well, what does that mean?' he says.

'They announced it on the p.a.' Sally says.

'Well, I didn't hear it' O'Connor says.

Sally sighs and looks into the distance.

'Anyway, Jerry's riding her' she says.

John O'Connor stares at her in disbelief.

'Jerry Chapman?!' he shouts.

Sally nods.

'Oh shit! Shit! You have got to be kidding' he says. 'He still claims three kilos in the country! He hasn't even ridden in town before!'

Though disappointed herself that the job is to be entrusted to such an inexperienced young rider, Sally rises to the boy's defence.

'He's ridden in town before' she says.

'When?' O'Connor snaps.

'Once, I think' she says. 'Anyway, at least we know he'll be trying.'

'Oh Jesus, what the hell happened to Shearer anyway?' John says.

Irritated, Sally bends down and pulls a brush from the tangle of gear in the bag.

'I don't know' she says, stroking the mare's mane.

CHAPTER 26

Jerry Chapman sits alone in the Jockeys' Room.

His fellow riders sort through their gear, step in and out of the sauna and weigh themselves on a set of scales, as he studies Star Chaser's race form.

4th of 18 Caulfield Cup, 2400 metres, Group One, 52kg, track slow, 1.8 lengths. T. Holt.

1st of 15 Turnbull Stakes, 2000 metres, Group Two, 53kg, track good, 2 lengths. T. Holt.

To the left of the bold capital letters spelling his mount's name is a small, coloured illustration depicting the same set of silks that now adorn his torso, covering the borrowed safety vest that grips him uncomfortably under the arms.

Jerry Chapman has no reason to be nervous. An outstanding rider, he has won countless big races in his mind, while he mucked out boxes and rode track work, often guiding his mounts through needle eye openings to hit the front in the shadows of the post. A genius in the saddle, confident and gifted, his many acceptance speeches are gracious and eloquent. Always acknowledging the race club committees and thanking owners, trainers and sponsors alike.

He lifts his head, takes a deep breath and looks up at a clock on the wall.

In forty minutes, Jerry Chapman, the seventeen year old from Mornington, the apprentice jockey still eligible for a three kilogram allowance in the country, will ride Star Chaser in the Melbourne Cup.

Soon to be pitted against the best riders in the country, in the most prestigious event on the calendar, he sits alone fumbling at the pages of his race book.

'Good luck kid' says a voice standing above him.

'Thanks' he says, looking up and shaking the hand jockey Keith Smith has extended towards him.

'You'll be right once you get out there' Smith says.

'You just have to go through a bit of rubbish beforehand.'

'Right' he says nodding.

Jerry assumes 'the bit of rubbish' is the pre-race mounting yard ceremony, where each horse's jockey is introduced to the crowd and perhaps the pre-race stewards' briefing.

No sooner has Smith walked away, the Jockeys' Room is once again a hive of activity, as the riders return from the cup curtain raiser, wearing their colourful silks and carrying saddles, caps and whips.

Jerry looks up, trying to catch Tommy Holt's eye, as the familiar voice of Jack Morgan calls out from the doorway.

'Jerry. You right son!' Jack says.

Jack's voice evokes a warmth and confidence that settles the boy's trembling nerves, if only momentarily.

He zips up his safety vest, buttons his silks and lifts his

gear from the bench. Careful to include his number twenty one saddlecloth and the pouch of lead weights he had so carefully measured a few minutes before.

Mr. Morgan is standing with an official and next to an antiquated jockey scale. Jerry steps onto the scales, as a slender black arrow swings back and forth, settling at a point that confirms he, together with saddle and gear, weighs fifty one and a half kilograms.

'J. Chapman, fifty one a half!' the official calls.

Jerry steps off the scales and passes the saddle across.

'Are you right with that Mr. Morgan?' he says.

'It's fine lad' Jack says.

Jack turns to walk away then stops and looks over his shoulder.

'I'll go and saddle her up and be back to have a chat alright?' he says.

'Yes sir' Jerry says.

Jack shuffles out of the scales area and stands on the veranda above the mounting yard, careful not to walk in front of the film crew recording an interview with a confident Len Lewis who is busy declaring Lord Melbery 'Close to a good thing.'

'Better have something on' Jack mutters, as he negotiates a route behind the camera and along the path leading away from the mounting yard.

Thousands of people are gathered either side of where the Melbourne Cup field will make its way to the Mounting Yard from the Birdcage enclosure. Members to the left and public to the right, each barricaded by rose bushes in full bloom. Many are already securing vantage points to watch the race, while others mill around the four bookmakers doing a brisk trade on the lawn. Jack glances across, curious to see if his horse is the medium of the punter's support.

The rubber surface of the path brings a spring to Jack's shuffling steps, as an attendant ushers him through a gate. He must now travel a distance of some forty metres through a swelling crowd to the relative obscurity and sanctuary of stall 115.

Cans of beer and plastic champagne flutes traverse his path, as he plots a route to the right of the gourmet sausage caravan and around the cypress hedge bordering the Birdcage.

Sally looks up as her father rounds the corner, the number 21 draped beneath the saddle he cradles on his arm.

He steps into an adjoining stall and lifts the saddle up to rest on a timber railing, as Sally moves over to help.

'What's happened Dad?' she asks.

Jack looks at Sally and John O'Connor.

'Colin Shearer passed out in the sauna. He's in hospital. The stewards reckon no one could make the weight and we would have to scratch her. So I've had to put the boy on.'

'You're kidding' O'Connor says.

'No I'm not' Jack says bluntly, laying a towel across the mare's back.

'I'll do it' Sally says, neatly folding the towel in place.

She picks up the saddle and places it on the mare's back.

'It's a bloody merry go round of jockeys that's for sure' Jack says.

John O'Connor says nothing.

Jack looks across at him. 'Cheer up' he says. 'Nobody died.'

* * * * * *

A long low platform sits in the centre of the Flemington mounting yard, covering many of the colourful sponsor logos painted onto the grass.

A single microphone stands front and centre of the stage, behind it a presenter bellows extravagant introductions for each jockey, inviting them to step on stage and wave to the crowd.

Tommy Holt is introduced as 'the man who will pilot the favourite, Lord Melbery.' He steps up and raises both hands in the air, acknowledging the crowd's modest applause.

Each jockey is introduced in saddlecloth order, many discovering nick names they never knew they had.

Jerry Chapman is twenty first in line. He listens to the ripple of applause that accompanies each introduction, fearing a chorus of 'Who?!' will erupt when he is finally introduced.

'Number twenty one, replacing Colin Shearer aboard Star Chaser, the apprentice rider from Mornington, Jerry Chapman!'

Jerry steps on to the stage before his introduction is complete. He waves nervously, barely glancing at the crowd, relieved that his applause is at least comparable to most of his rivals.

The introductions complete, the jockeys waste no time in making their way back inside. Jerry trails behind, as a lone voice yells out from the crowd.

'Good on ya Jerry. Go you good thing!'

Jerry tries to act calm and aloof, before his foot becomes tangled in a television cable, hurriedly being dragged across his path.

The cable lassoes his ankle, forcing him to hop sideways, as a cameraman blindly tugs at his leg.

Embarrassed, he eventually manages to escape the trap, while waving away a pall of smoke that billows in his face.

Jerry pushes past the gathering press, as Albert Maressmo puffs on a cigar.

CHAPTER 27

Fred and Beryl Chapman sit together on a couch in their lounge room, surrounded by some thirty people. Beryl bounces up and down, pointing excitedly at the television every time Star Chaser appears in shot.

Sally Morgan leads the mare around the mounting yard. A tiny, borrowed saddle strapped around the chestnut's ample girth. A saddle that will carry the seventeen year old apprentice Jerry Chapman, together with the hopes and dreams of an ageing trainer, an excited owner, several punters and the entire population of Mornington.

Twenty four jockeys, fresh from their pre-race briefing with the stewards, wander across the mounting yard, amidst a multitude of owners, trainers, journalists, television crews and officials, in search of their respective connections.

Tommy Holt shakes hands with Len Lewis and Albert Maressmo, turning his back to Jack Morgan not ten feet away.

Jerry Chapman shakes hands with Jack and nods hello to John O'Connor.

Jack glances across the mounting yard, as Sally leads the mare on another lap.

'Now son' Jack says, 'don't worry if you're nervous. We are all nervous and there isn't a jockey in the race that isn't.'

Jerry looks at Mr. Morgan and nods. His arms are folded across his chest. White knuckles grip his whip.

Jack continues. 'Now we've drawn a good alley and it's important that we use it.'

John O'Connor, mildly offended he is not credited with the favourable, if entirely random barrier draw, stands with his hands in his pockets saying nothing.

'I don't want you to hunt her out of the gates, but make sure she's running' Jack says. 'I want to see her just off the pace, about fifth or sixth passing the post the first time. Now a couple are sure to be caught wide and they're going to want to press forward so if you're not careful you can get shuffled back.'

Jerry hangs on every word as Sally and Star Chaser complete another lap.

'Most importantly' Jack says 'let her find her own pace and her own rhythm. Don't try to fight with her, she will only get stirred up. It's crucial that you get her to settle. She has to relax okay.'

Jerry concentrates on the key words in Mr. Morgan's instruction. Just off the pace, settle, relax.

His mental filing cabinet is filling fast, as Mr. Morgan continues.

'Now most of all, be patient. You can bet some of these blokes will be taking off too early and be spent before the turn. You are going to have to wait for the last crack at them.'

'Thank you riders mount up!' the chief steward shouts,

as twenty four small conferences start to break up.

Jack and Jerry walk over to the corner of the mounting yard where Sally has led Star Chaser, leaving John O'Connor standing alone.

'You want to hit the front at the clock tower son. That's about a furlong out' Jack adds, resting his hand on the boy's shoulder.

Sally holds the mare up on a small corner of grass, thinking her father has probably spoken more words to Jerry in the last five minutes than throughout his entire tenure with the stable.

Jerry reaches up and pulls down a stirrup iron.

'Good luck lad' Jack says, as he hoists him into the saddle.

Jerry fumbles his toes into the stirrups and holds the reins in his trembling hands, as Sally looks up smiling.

'Fancy seeing you here' she says.

'Yeah, fancy that' he says softly.

'She's been really good' Sally says, 'so quiet.'

'That's good' Jerry says, 'because I'm terrified.'

Sally leads the mare around the Mounting Yard again. Earlier she had maintained a position in saddlecloth order, behind number twenty Rochester and ahead of number twenty two, Hat Stand. Now each runner has its jockey aboard and the order is largely random. Sally, Jerry and Star Chaser find themselves parading directly behind Lord Melbery with Tommy Holt in the saddle, the sun glistening off the creases in his jet black silks.

'There you go' Sally says, 'just stay on his tail the whole way and you won't go far wrong.'

A trumpet fanfare sounds, as the clerk of the course, leads the top weight, Prince Akabah down the narrow race that leads onto the track. The rest of the field follows, each horse led by its handler, past a sea of people pressed against the fence.

Sally leads the mare down the race, as Jerry faces away from the crowd mulling over Mr. Morgan's instructions.

'Be up on the pace but get her to settle' already a contradiction. 'Ride her quietly and get her to relax.'

Jerry feels his hands tremble and his stomach churn. He will do well to ride her at all.

Sally leads the mare onto the track and unclips the lead rope from the bridle. She holds onto the reins just long enough to say 'Good luck' before Star Chaser breaks into a trot and with Jerry Chapman perched in the saddle the mare makes her way up the straight towards the starting stalls.

* * * * * *

'There he is!' Beryl cries, as the television cameras focus on her son aboard Star Chaser.

'Yes dear I can see him' Fred says, discouraging his wife's hand from strangling his knee.

The television commentators are generous enough to describe Jerry as 'a promising apprentice,' all the while acknowledging the fact he faces a huge task for one so young and inexperienced.

'Oh what would you know?' his mother counters.

'Yes, all right dear' Fred says calmly, as his wife shuffles forward in her seat.

Sally arrives in the mounting yard ignoring the wolf whistles and invitations from a handful of males in the crowd.

'Well she travelled down alright' she says to her father, as they peer into the distance.

'Just as well' Jack says, 'he looks as white as a sheet.'

'Let's just hope he sticks to the plan' John says.

'I'm not sure he even heard me' Jack mutters.

Sally points to the owner's section of the grandstand, as Albert Maressmo slides open the window of his private box.

* * * * * *

The Melbourne Cup field gathers behind the barriers.

Jerry Chapman pulls gently on his left rein and turns Star Chaser around. He looks up for the first time since Sally unclipped the lead rope, to see the massive crowd and packed grandstands.

His throat is instantly dry, his stomach leaps into his chest and his head spins. Before he even realises, he is lying face down on the turf. Confused and frightened he staggers to his feet, pressing his head and hands against the running rail. An attendant takes hold of the reins and another picks up his whip, as the contents of the boy's stomach lurch onto the ground.

'Are you right there mate?' an attendant asks.

Jerry coughs, splutters and spits on the grass. He wipes a tear from his eye and takes hold of his whip.

'I am alright' he says, 'thanks.'

'I think this one's yours' the attendant says, holding the

riderless chestnut's bridle.

Jack grips his binoculars unsteadily in one hand, masking a worried expression, as the race caller announces 'Now the boy's hopped out of the saddle on Star Chaser.'

'What's going on Dad?' Sally asks, as her father and John O'Connor focus their gaze.

'I can't see' Jack says, the binoculars draped around his neck. 'Here' he says, lifting them over his head and handing them to Sally, 'I can't hold the bloody things.'

Sally focuses on the activity behind the barriers.

By the time she finds Star Chaser, Jerry is back aboard and the field is being called in.

'It's alright Dad' she says excitedly, 'I can see her.'

Sally, Jack and John are seated in the front row of the owner's section, some two hundred metres ahead of the finish and directly opposite a giant video screen.

Fred and Beryl Chapman lean forward on the couch, surrounded by friends.

Albert Maressmo and Len Lewis enjoy the comforts of a private box, while Colin Shearer lies in a hospital bed, nursing a saline drip in his arm.

Inspector Frank Dennis is nowhere to be seen but in all probability amongst the crowd somewhere.

MELBOURNE CUP FIELD

1. PRINCE AKABAH (17)
2. LORD MELBERY (13)
3. LAUGHING CLOWNS (5)
4. EURODOLLAR (9)
5. THE BANKER (2)
6. VENETIAN (11)
7. NORTHERN LIGHTS (4)
8. ALBARAK (18)
9. SKY BLUE ARMY (22)
10. INSTANT REPLAY (14)
11. STYLUS (21)
12. SIR ROCCO (19)
13. BAY STREET (15)
14. FARGONE (8)
15. RISE 'N' SHINE (6)
16. BARBENSHANK (10)
17. GARGARELLE (1)
18. TOWN HALL (23)
19. PRIDE OF KILLARNEY (3)
20. ROCHESTER (20)
21. STAR CHASER (7)
22. HAT STAND (24)
23. LOMBARD (12)
24. GOLDEN PALACE (16)

CHAPTER 28

A helicopter hovers overhead, as the first of the twenty four Melbourne Cup runners are led into the barriers.

Jerry Chapman doesn't dare look up at the grandstands. It is all he can do not to jump off his horse and hide beneath one of the thousands of cars parked in the centre of the course.

The gates fill steadily, as he walks his mount in a circle. Gargarelle stands in one, The Banker in two and Pride of Killarney in three. Jerry glances across to see Tommy Holt walk Lord Melbery into barrier thirteen, as an attendant takes hold of the Star Chaser's bridle, leading her in to barrier seven. The mare walks in and stands quietly, turning her head to see Fargone join the line on her outside. More than half the field is loaded, as Jerry drags a pair of goggles down from his cap. He picks up the reins, leans forward and whispers in Star Chaser's ear 'Look after me Rosie.'

Jack Morgan's eyes fix to the giant screen on the inside of the track. Sally and John train their binoculars on the start. Fred and Beryl Chapman hold hands on the couch.

The starter mounts a platform behind the inside rail. He

flicks a switch and an amber coloured light flashes atop the barriers. The field is set.

Jerry Chapman is shaking, as he studies the gap in the barrier closed shut in front of him.

'Hold on sir!' a jockey cries from the outside. Town Hall is rearing up and an attendant climbs into the gates to settle the horse again.

All the while, Jerry Chapman breathes deeply.

The racecourse falls silent.

The caller announces 'They're set for a start in the Melbourne Cup.'

The starter studies the line.

Jerry firmly grips the reins, as the barriers crash open to the cheers of the crowd.

Star Chaser launches herself out of the gates.

The field is spread across the track, with several horses on the mare's outside already ahead of her.

Jerry recalls Mr. Morgan's instructions.

'Make sure she is up on the pace.'

He sits down in the saddle, pushing with his arms and shoulders. The mare responds and holds her position. Rise 'n' Shine, the horse drawn on her inside is behind her, as Jerry angles his mount towards the fence. Pride of Killarney is a length in front and aiming to lead, as Jerry steers the mare behind Northern Lights. Horses are cutting across from out wide and Star Chaser cops a heavy bump that throws her off stride, but helps to position her against the rail three lengths from the lead.

The runners gallop down the Flemington straight, as

more and more horses cross from the outside. Jerry has Star Chaser locked away on the fence and no option other than to sit tight and watch, as Pride of Killarney hands up to Sir Rocco and it in turn to Sky Blue Army, before Town Hall slides across and into lead, with the winning post fast approaching.

Star Chaser is shuffled back to a position midfield and as the pace slackens, Jerry pulls on the reins trying to slow the mare, for fear she may clip the heels of the horse in front.

Cramped for room and resenting the strain of the bit in her mouth, she tosses her head, fighting her rider, as the field travels past the owners' section of the grandstand.

'Leave her alone son!' Jack cries, as the field gallops by. His eyes dart back to the giant screen to see his jockey tugging on the reins and the mare laying her ears back.

Jerry starts to panic, he is already well back in the field and his mount will have soon run her race if she doesn't settle down.

His mind flashes back to his track work fall. How he got to his feet, just in time to see his boss knocked off his and what he would give not to let Mr. Morgan down - again.

As the field turns out of the straight, the pace quickens and Jerry can give the mare more rein. She lowers her head and starts to relax. The boy loosens his grip and whispers in her ear 'Easy girl, easy.' He looks at the horses around him. He is trailing directly behind Northern Lights. Ahead of him are the black and red silks of Lord Melbery, behind him is The Banker, then Prince Akabah and on his outside, caught three wide is Stylus.

Jack, Sally and John sit silent in the stand, concentrating on the race. Jack studies the pace, not concerned the mare is well back, as the speed is on and the leaders are likely to tire.

The Chapman's lounge room comes alive, each time the camera sweeps through the field, past the rangy chestnut camped on the fence, with Mornington's own in the saddle.

The field gallops towards the back of the course. With half the journey completed, Jerry whispers 'Good girl, good girl' as Star Chaser travels sweetly. He remembers how Mr. Morgan told him to be patient, to save her for the last crack. All the same he looks ahead at the favourites, Lord Melbery and Prince Akabah and wonders how he is going to avoid being blocked on the rails, as Laughing Clowns moves up on his outside.

The field passes the 1200 metre mark and some jockeys are starting to make their move. Jerry can see Tommy Holt sitting quietly on Lord Melbery, as more and more horses gather around him.

The mare is travelling easily, as others start to feel the pinch, but as the field swings for home she is buried in the pack.

The rider on Northern Lights feels for his whip, his mount is starting to struggle, but Star Chaser is pocketed with Laughing Clowns travelling well on her outside. Jerry looks up to see Tommy Holt edging closer to the lead, as Prince Akabah takes up the running.

The field straightens for the run home, 600 metres out and Jerry can hear the noise of the crowd.

Jack Morgan shuffles in his seat, his eyes switching from

the giant screen to the field heading for home.

'Where is he?!' Beryl cries from the couch.

'There behind them!' Fred shouts, pointing at the television, as cheers of 'Come on Jerry!' propel from the back of the room.

500 metres to run and Star Chaser is stuck behind the tiring Northern Lights, desperately searching for a way out.

The race caller confirms the dilemma.

"And further back to Star Chaser in need of a run."

Jack Morgan leaps to his feet. 'Get her out son!' he screams.

The mare is travelling like a winner but has nowhere to go.

Jerry searches for the black and red silks of Lord Melbery. Tommy Holt has set sail for home and is already four lengths ahead.

His head darts from side to side. To his left is the rail, to his right, the grey Lombard and ahead, Northern Lights threatens to fall in his lap.

Slowly the grey horse drops back and he can ease the mare off the heels of the tiring outsider.

300 metres to run and Lord Melbery claims Prince Akabah, with Laughing Clowns closing fast.

Star Chaser is seventh but full of running, as horses tire around her.

Suddenly, Prince Akabah starts to weaken and a gap opens up. Jerry wrestles his mount towards it and the mare bursts through into clear ground, the leaders in her sights.

Jerry Chapman is stunned. He can see the packed

grandstands and hear the roar of the crowd, with just five horses ahead of him and the clock tower looming large.

Star Chaser has put herself into the race, but now it's up to him.

He gathers the reins and digs his toes into the stirrups. Gripping her shoulder with his knees, he hurls the mare forward, yelling 'Get home girl!'

His parent's lounge room explodes, as Jack, Sally and John O'Connor shout as one.

Star Chaser gains ground quickly. She moves to third, then second behind Lord Melbery. Tommy Holt is hurling his whip at the favourite, smacking its rump with every stride.

Jerry steadies his head over the mare's neck and rides her with all the strength he can muster.

At that moment, his nerves disappear and his fear dissolves.

For the first time he believes he can win.

He has to win.

For Jack, for Sal, for Mum, for Dad.

With every beat of the mare's action, he begs her to raise another effort.

For Jack, For Sal, for Mum, for Dad.

As each hoof strikes the turf.

For Jack, for Sal, for Mum for Dad.

100 metres to run and Star Chaser is half a length astern of Lord Melbery, gaining ground with every stride.

For Jack, for Sal, for Mum for Dad.

50 metres to run and a neck separates them.

For Jack, for Sal, for Mum for Dad.

A stride before the post and Star Chaser draws level.

The noise of the crowd is deafening but Jerry Chapman hears nothing. He shuts his eyes, grits his teeth and throws his mount at the line.

CHAPTER 29

The huge crowd cheers and applauds, though few if any can tell which horse has won.

As the last few runners cross the finish, a lone journalist strides into the centre of the mounting yard, dictating copy over a mobile phone.

'Seventeen year old apprentice, Jerry Chapman rode the perfect race aboard Star Chaser, the race of his young life. He had passion in his hands, God in his heart and a head to spare when they hit the line.'

A close up image of the finish on both the giant screen and television monitors confirms that Star Chaser has indeed got the better of Lord Melbery. It is a visual cue for raucous celebrations.

Sally bursts into tears and throws her arms around her father. John O'Connor stands with both fists punching the air, while a modest lounge room above a corner shop in Mornington spirals into a collective delirium.

Jerry Chapman slumps over his mount's neck, as the mare winds down, cantering past a row of corporate marquees.

'Oh my God! Oh my God!' his mother cries, her body

shaking, as tears stream down her cheeks. She steadies herself on her husband's shoulder, as Fred shakes dozens of hands and accepts a succession of pats on the back. Behind him a champagne cork bursts from a bottle, hurling above his head and across the room.

Jack Morgan shuffles to the top of the stairs that lead down to the mounting yard. He grips the rail in his hand and with legs of jelly, plants both feet on each step, as he slowly descends. Sally and John have raced ahead and are waiting at the entrance to the mounting yard for Star Chaser to return.

John puts his arm around Sally and points to the giant screen on the inside of the track, where the number twenty one is displayed in first place.

Most of the field has returned and waits opposite the winning post, as Jerry canters Star Chaser along the outside rail, lapping up the attention from various picnics dotted around the course.

Generous applause greets a beaming jockey aboard the winner, as he parades his mount before the crowd.

The clerk of the course escorts Star Chaser along a rose lined race towards the mounting yard and past thousands of cheering fans. Jerry can see Sally and John waiting for him as he looks up at the grandstands, waving to the crowd.

Sally is crying, as she clips a lead onto the mare's bridle, while John O'Connor slaps a hand on the boy's thigh yelling 'Good on ya buddy!'

Jerry discovers new reserves of energy, becoming quite the showman, as he stands in the saddle, twirling his whip and punching the air.

Sally leads the mare back to scale through a swarm of photographers and television cameras, as Jerry leans down saying 'We did it Sal.'

'You did it Jerry' she says.

Jack Morgan is surrounded by a sea of reporters and cameras, as Star Chaser arrives in the winner's enclosure. Anxious to greet his horse, he pushes past the place getters to congratulate his jockey.

The rolling mall rushes past Lord Melbery's connections and gathers around the heaving, perspiring frame of Star Chaser. The mare's neck is a lather of sweat and steam billows from her hide, as Jerry Chapman unbuckles the girth strap and drags the saddle from her back. All the while he is asked to tell the world 'how it feels to win a Melbourne Cup at your first attempt?'

'Well done son' Jack says, choking back tears.

'Thanks Mr. Morgan' Jerry says, as he skips inside carrying his saddle. He steps onto the jockey scale, handing his whip and cap to chief steward Jim Cutler.

An official reads aloud from a race book.

'Star Chaser. Fifty one and a half.'

Jerry turns his head towards the large clock face atop the scales. He holds his breath, as a black metal arrow swings and bounces between fifty one and fifty two kilograms.

'Righto' the chief steward says, handing him his cap and whip. Jerry wastes no time stepping off, allowing Tommy Holt to weigh in.

'Went the wrong way Tom?' Cutler says, as the scales confirm Lord Melbery has carried his allotted handicap.

Tommy Holt says nothing.

Jerry runs into the Jockeys' Room. He throws his borrowed saddle down, bursts into the bathroom and jumps up and down, yelling deliriously at his own reflection.

Sally backs the mare out of the winner's enclosure and walks her around the mounting yard, amidst the connections of the also rans.

'Correct weight. All clear on the Melbourne Cup' is announced over the public address system, as a satin rug is draped over the winner.

A mobile stage is rolled into position, while sponsor signage and microphones are hurriedly erected. The mare paws the ground impatiently, as her rug is tied in place. A spectacular gold trophy is removed from a timber box and placed in the centre of a table, as a burly security guard stands by.

Jack Morgan is learning to cope with his new found celebrity. He insists he did not fall out with Tommy Holt and that while he was certainly disappointed when Colin Shearer became indisposed, he always had faith in his young apprentice and that 'yes' this is by far his greatest moment in racing.

Jerry jogs across the grass, still wearing his white, black and yellow silks. His hair is wet and crudely parted, as he joins Jack Morgan and John O'Connor. He shakes John's hand and hugs Mr. Morgan, as Sally leads Star Chaser behind the stage.

Sir Donald Simpson stands amidst a gathering of sponsors, officials, promotional staff and dignitaries, addressing the crowd and a worldwide television audience, as Jerry smiles and waves at Sally.

CHAPTER 30

While most racegoers leave Flemington in the comfort of air conditioned motor cars, winning Melbourne Cup jockey Jerry Chapman rides home in the back of Jack Morgan's three tonne truck, with a five year old chestnut mare and a mobile phone for company.

He sits on a fold out stool and try as he may he cannot keep still. He recalls the race over and over in his mind, with subtle variations gracing each recollection. As the truck rolls around each corner, he leans across, angling away from the rail to make his run. He slaps his thigh with the palm of his hand, again and again in an extravagant whipping action, even though he never once pulled the stick on Star Chaser.

The press had been complimentary of his patient, confident ride. How he was happy to ride the mare out hands and heels and not use the whip. The fact is he was so overawed at the time he didn't even think to use it. Let the world believe what it wants. In any case, it wouldn't have mattered. Star Chaser gave everything she had in the last hundred metres and more besides. More than could be gained from a belt on the backside.

Ahead in the cabin Jack sits in the passenger seat, feeling no pain. Sally aims the truck down a straight stretch of highway, as her father releases thirty thousand dollars' worth of hand crafted gold from a felt lined, timber box.

'Gosh it's heavy' he says smiling, 'must be the real thing.'

Sally glances across, as her father stares at the trophy cradled in his lap. 'Just don't drop it' she says.

'I won't drop it' he says. 'I have spent my whole life dreaming of winning this. I'm not about to put a dint in it!'

Sally laughs, stares at the highway and winds the truck up to ninety.

* * * * * *

'Just hang it on the corner there and bung a bit of tape on it.'

No one could be sure when local publican Mike Roberts last took charge of decorating the Royal Hotel with streamers and balloons. Yet the overweight fifty year old appears to be making a good fist of it.

He stands at the base of a ladder, his wife Mavis perched four rungs high, surrounded by an array of black, white and yellow decorations. Streamers are weaved around light fittings and ceiling fans, while clusters of balloons are taped to picture frames and door trims. A cardboard replica Melbourne Cup trophy is covered in gold foil and stuck to the wall above the entrance to the bistro.

The pub is doing a roaring trade for a Tuesday night and for the first time in its history, is catering to three television news crews, amongst hundreds of regulars and town's folk, all awaiting the arrival of the newly indentured local heroes.

Mavis carries the ladder behind the bar and down into the cellar, as Mike pulls another beer and listens to more outrageous lies of his customer's punting successes.

John O'Connor swings the front door open and ushers the Morgans and Chapmans inside, as Mike reaches for an antique brass bell (normally used to herald the result of the Monday night meat tray raffle), ringing it furiously.

The crowd's attention turns to the bar and then to the door, as Jack Morgan holds the Melbourne Cup trophy aloft.

A huge roar erupts, as dozens rush over, anxious to be among the first to congratulate the victors.

Star Chaser's connections are bathed in powerful spotlights, as the television crews seek to capture the moment.

Jack makes his way to the bar, planting the trophy down on a moist cotton towel.

'Good on ya Jack' Mike says boisterously, shaking the trainer's hand so hard his head shakes. 'There you go' he adds, as a cold glass of beer is thrust in front of him.

Mavis skips from behind the bar and plants a kiss on his cheek. 'Look at you Jack' she says. 'You're famous now.'

We'll all be famous in a minute' Jack says, pointing to the cameras.

Mike has taken charge of the trophy and promptly fills it with beer, passing it over the bar for his patrons to sample.

'Does it taste any different?' he says, laughing heartily.

In the midst of the mayhem, Jerry Chapman is smothered.

A teenage hero surrounded by a host of people more than twice his age, ruffling his hair, slapping his back and shaking his hand. He thanks each one, though he can't recall ever having met most of them.

John O'Connor is not well known amongst the locals and stays close to Sally.

'Hey turn it up!' someone shouts from in front of the bar, as a news update is televised on a monitor mounted to the wall.

The crowd falls silent as the presenter explains 'a record crowd attended today's Melbourne Cup' before introducing a replay of the race.

Mike points a remote control at the monitor, increasing the volume to the point of distortion, as the field jumps away.

Beryl Chapman stands with her arm around her son, as the field passes the winning post the first time. Cheers ebb and flow, as the camera tracks through the field, the crowd finding full voice, as Star Chaser storms home and hits the line.

Fred Chapman wipes tears from his eyes, as his wife sobs and hugs their son.

The television shows pictures of the return to scale, with the presenter explaining a more comprehensive coverage of the event will feature later in the bulletin.

Everyone's attention is drawn away from the television and back to the celebrations with renewed vigour.

Everyone, with the exception of John O'Connor.

He stands looking up at the monitor. On the screen and

behind the presenter's left shoulder is a photograph of Alan Da Silva. Underneath his portrait are the words 'Murder Investigation.'

There has been a breakthrough in the case. While the Melbourne Cup was run this afternoon, Victorian police raided a suburban house, taking possession of a late model black Lexus. Forensic tests have revealed it is the same car used in the recent hit and run slaying of the famous jockey.

'John O'Connor?' says a voice standing behind the winning owner.

O'Connor stands with his head bowed. His hand clutching the keys to the rental car he has been driving for the past week, while his own stayed locked in his garage, nursing a cracked windscreen and damaged front end.

Sally looks across the crowd, peering through a sea of heads, curious why two uniformed policeman and a third man, dressed in a suit are standing with John.

Inspector Frank Dennis extends his left arm and takes hold of O'Connor's right.

'Can you come with us please?' he says.

CHAPTER 31

John O'Connor, fresh from a night in the cells, sits next to his solicitor in an interview room at the St. Kilda Road police station. Inspector Frank Dennis sits opposite, his hands resting on a folder, as Detective Constable Melanie Wilson sits down.

'This much we know' Dennis says. 'Yesterday afternoon, we conducted a search of your home, where our officers uncovered a motor vehicle. A vehicle registered in your name and owned by you. A vehicle that we believe killed Alan Da Silva.'

O'Connor says nothing, as Dennis opens the folder and removes a piece of paper.

'We also found this document. Do you recognise it?'

O'Connor looks at his solicitor, who nods.

'Yes' he says.

'This document is signed by you and dated August 3rd 2018. It is a credit betting agreement between yourself and Crown Casino. Is that correct?'

'Yes' O'Connor says.

'An agreement you personally secured with Albert Maressmo?' Dennis says.

O'Connor says nothing.

'Well you both signed it' Dennis says, raising his voice.

'Yes' O'Connor replies.

'Now let me tell you what else we know' Dennis says.

O'Connor folds his arms across his chest and leans back in his chair.

'This document allows you to bet at the casino and generate losses of up to $100,000' Dennis says. 'It also grants the other party to the agreement, in this case Albert Maressmo, the right to seize any otherwise unsecured asset of yours in the event that monies in excess of the specified limit are not repaid within 30 days. Are you aware of that?'

'Yes' O'Connor says.

Dennis takes another piece of paper from the file and slides it across the table.

'John, your account has shown a debit balance of nearly $300,000 for the past six months' Dennis says.

'Yes' O'Connor says.

'That's a pretty unhealthy situation, wouldn't you say?' Dennis says.

'Yes' O'Connor says.

'We also know' Dennis says 'that Alan Da Silva owed the casino over $400,000 and that he was trying to blackmail Maressmo into writing off the debt by threatening to blow the whistle on last year's race fix.

'Is that so?' O'Connor says.

'Now, let me tell you what I think happened' Dennis says, 'Maressmo has you by the balls with this debt. You're $180,000 over your limit and he is poised to exercise his right to seize ownership of Star Chaser just days before she runs in the Melbourne Cup. Then, all of a sudden, he offers to forget the whole thing, to wipe out the debt and leave Star Chaser in your hands, if you will do him this one small favour.'

O'Connor says nothing.

'Maressmo calls you up and says Da Silva is in the casino' Dennis says. 'He tells you where he parks his car. You drive over there and wait. You see him leave. You see him walk towards his car and the rest, as they say, is history. Your debt is cleared, you keep the ownership of your racehorse and Maressmo has fixed his problem. Everybody wins.'

O'Connor turns and looks at his solicitor.

'Inspector, perhaps I might have a moment to consult with my client' she says.

* * * * * *

Jack and Sally Morgan sit together in their lounge room watching television, as a journalist files a live report from outside their property.

The Melbourne Cup trophy sits on the mantelpiece and the phone off the hook, as the reporter confirms John O'Connor has been arrested by police but not yet charged.

His detention had brought their celebrations to a premature end. There was no frantic chase, no tearful confession and above all no explanation. John O'Connor said nothing at all as he was led away, leaving the Morgans, the Chapmans and much of Mornington to piece the puzzle together.

* * * * * *

O'Connor's solicitor beckons the two investigating officers into the interview room.

'Inspector, my client would like to make a statement' she says.

Dennis looks at O'Connor.

'Well, let's hear it then' he says.

O'Connor leans forward, holding a sheet of paper in his hands. He stares at his handwritten prose, takes a deep breath and passes it to his solicitor, who reads aloud.

Wednesday November 6th 2019

In July last year, I met Albert Maressmo during a celebration dinner at Crown Casino. Maressmo presented me with several hundred dollars' worth of gambling chips and later that evening he offered me a credit betting account with the casino. You have a copy of this agreement in your possession.

I began betting on account with the casino and continued to wager and lose increasing sums of money, to the point where my account was frozen in April this year with a debit balance of $283,450.

I have been unable to repay this debt, as I have continued to incur substantial losses with various bookmakers and with the TAB.

In October this year I received a telephone call from Mr. Maressmo, asking me to attend a meeting at his office. During the course of our conversation he explained that he had a proposal whereby I could repay my debt in full.

I attended the meeting on Monday October 21st at

6.00pm. Mr. Maressmo and I were the only people present.

Mr. Maressmo said he intended to exercise his right to seize ownership of my racehorse Star Chaser, if I did not repay $283,450 immediately.

I could not pay and having already lost my family, I panicked at the prospect of losing ownership of my racehorse.

Mr. Maressmo then explained that he needed someone to sort out a problem he had with Alan Da Silva and he offered to write off my entire debt if I agreed to kill him.

At first I refused, but my racehorse is my life and the prospect of seeing her run in the Melbourne Cup in Maressmo's ownerships was more than I could bear. I felt I had no choice and agreed to his terms.

I received a telephone call from Mr. Maressmo late at night on Thursday October 31ˢ. He explained Da Silva was playing blackjack in the casino. He said he was alone, described what he was wearing and where he had parked his car.

I drove to the casino, parked nearby and waited for Da Silva to leave.

He left the casino and entered the car park at approximately 4.00am. As he did, I accelerated and ran him down. I then drove home where I received a telephone call from Mr. Maressmo some hours later. He said I no longer had anything to worry about and that I owed him nothing.

O'Connor's solicitor passes his statement across the table.

Dennis lifts a corner of the page and looks up.

'Was anyone else present at any stage when you met with Maressmo?' he says.

'No' O'Connor says.

'But someone must have seen you there surely, a receptionist or a secretary?' Dennis says.

'Well, yes' O'Connor says, 'one or two others I suppose.'

'So we can prove a meeting took place' Dennis says.

'I suppose. What does that mean for me?' O'Connor says.

'Well it marries with your statement' Dennis says 'and if you can prove Maressmo coerced you into doing what you did, together with the fact you have made a full confession. Well, it's a matter for the court really.'

'Right' O'Connor says.

'It's Maressmo we want' Dennis says. 'He probably thinks he's untouchable, but if you're willing to help us, we might be able to make a case.'

'And what do I get?' O'Connor says.

'Well as I said, it's a matter for the court' Dennis says. 'I can't promise anything, but do you really want to wear this whole thing on your own?'

'No, I don't' O'Connor says.

'Okay fine. Here's what we do' Dennis says. 'We will release you on your own undertaking and draft a statement to the effect that you have not been charged. As far as the press are concerned you are simply helping us with our enquiries. Two officers will escort you home this morning and deliver you to me this afternoon outside Crown Casino. We'll see if we can get you in to see Maressmo. We will fit you with a wire, so any conversation will be recorded. Is that clear?'

O'Connor nods.

'And you are okay with that?' Dennis says.

'Yes. Yes I am' O'Connor says.

CHAPTER 32

John O'Connor returns home, he has a shower and changes his clothes, all the while facing the prospect of confronting Albert Maressmo, while Inspector Frank Dennis listens and records their conversation.

A uniformed constable ushers him into the back seat of an unmarked car, before they drive to Melbourne's south bank landmark.

He meets Dennis in the back of a plain white van surrounded by an array of recording equipment, as a technician fits a wire and microphone under his shirt.

'Now' Dennis says. 'It's very important that we get him to agree that your original meeting took place. Try to confirm the date and time if you can. This equipment is very sensitive, so just speak normally and try not to brush against anything or fold your arms across your chest.'

'Right' O'Connor says.

'We will hear and record everything that is said, okay?' Dennis says.

'Sure' O'Connor replies.

'Off you go then' Dennis says 'and good luck.'

O'Connor steps out of the van and walks towards a glass tower that houses the casino offices. He walks into the foyer, up a grand, sweeping staircase and takes an elevator to the third floor, where a young female receptionist sits behind a long white desk.

'Hello' he says. 'My name is John O'Connor. I would like to speak with Mr. Maressmo.'

'Do you have an appointment sir?' she asks.

'No I don't' he says.

'May I ask what it's regarding?' she says.

'It's of a personal nature' he says.

'Okay' she says and picks up a handset. 'What was your name again?'

'John O'Connor' he says.

The receptionist speaks quietly for a few seconds and hangs up the phone.

'I'm sorry sir' she says 'but Mr. Maressmo can't see you at the moment. Perhaps you would like to leave a card?'

'Tell him it is John O'Connor' he says.

'I did' she says.

'Well tell him again' he says sternly.

She picks up the handset once more and says 'Perhaps you would like to take a seat.'

O'Connor sits down and waits before Tiffany Kirk-Jones strides into the reception area. She in turn is directed towards the man sitting in the black leather arm chair.

'Mr. O'Connor' she says. 'My name is Tiffany Kirk-Jones, how do you do?'

Dennis rolls his eyes, as he listens in the van.

'I'm afraid Mr. Maressmo is not available at the moment, but perhaps I can help?'

O'Connor stands.

'Perhaps you can' he says.

Frank Dennis looks towards his audio technician, curious why the conversation has stalled, save for the odd, short stabbing cry and muffled sound of some thing, or some one brushing against the microphone.

'He's not kissing her is he?' the technician ponders.

'Dennis can hear the PR manager's breath racing, her voice stuttered and paralysed with fear.

'Jesus Christ!' Dennis cries, as he bursts out of the van and sprints towards the building.

John O'Connor clenches a mass of bright red hair in his left fist. His right grips a hand gun, the point of its barrel pressed under his victim's chin.

Dennis bursts into the building.

'Office?!' he bellows, thrusting his ID badge in the face of a bemused employee. 'Maressmo's office?!'

A uniformed security guard greets John O'Connor and Tiffany Kirk-Jones as the elevator doors open on the sixth floor.

'Door!' O'Connor shouts.

The guard obliges.

'Where's the bloody lift?' Dennis protests, pressing the 'up' button again and again before the elevator doors finally slide open.

'Come on, come on' he pleads, as each floor number lights up in turn. Three, four, five…

Dennis races onto the sixth floor, where he finds a uniformed security guard consoling a hysterical Tiffany Kirk-Jones.

The guard points towards a thick timber door on the far side of a lavish foyer.

'Who's in there?' Dennis demands.

'Just the two of them, I think' the guard says, his response punctuated by the PR Manager's constant sobbing.

Dennis rushes over and stands with his face all but pressed against the door.

'John O'Connor! It's Frank Dennis!' he says.

He turns to the guard. 'Can he hear me?'

The guard shrugs his shoulders.

'John!' he shouts again. 'It's Frank Dennis! I'm going to open the door! I'm alone and I am unarmed!'

Dennis slowly turns a polished brass knob. He presses his hand against the door and feels the lock give way.

The door opens barely an inch.

'John, it's Frank Dennis' he says, 'I'm coming in. Just very slowly okay, very slowly.'

Dennis steps inside the office.

John O'Connor stands with his back to the door, in front of a large and solid timber desk.

Albert Maressmo slouches in an elaborate brown leather chair.

O'Connor alive, Maressmo dead.

Three shots have hit the casino boss in the chest. His white business shirt is stained bright red.

Dennis creeps forward, takes the gun from O'Connor's

hand, wraps it in a handkerchief and slips it into his jacket pocket, as Maressmo's body slides off its chair and flops on the floor beneath his desk.

CHAPTER 33

'Camped in front of the idiot box' is how Jack Morgan intends to spend Melbourne Cup Day this year, should anyone ask.

Sally will spend the day with her new boyfriend, while Star Chaser wanders the lush paddocks of a Hunter Valley stud farm, having recently been confirmed in foal. Her stud career, together with the performances of her progeny, will give her owner and breeder a lifelong interest - one to match his sentence.

Jerry Chapman has six rides at Wangaratta, preferring to honour commitments to the trainers and owners who have continued to support him, rather than accept the offer of a single ride at Flemington.

Frank Dennis' law enforcement career has been curtailed by the various enquiries that followed the search of John O'Connor's home. The search that failed to discover the hand gun he taped to his ankle before their ill-fated entrapment exercise at Crown Casino.

Dennis sits alone in his flat, seeking solace in cigarettes and alcohol.

'I'll see you later then Dad' Sally says, bending down to kiss her father on the cheek. 'You'll be alright on your own won't you?'

'Don't worry about me' he says, 'I'm not about to bet the farm on anything.'

Sally smiles, lifts the Melbourne Cup trophy from the mantelpiece and places it on top of the television.

'Might as well give the day a sense of occasion' she says.

'Sure, why not?' Jack says smiling, as the field is called in for the first.

A Note From The Author

Thank you for reading a copy of my book 'First Tuesday.'

It really is very humbling to think that someone would invest the time to read something I have written.

I hope you enjoyed it and if you did, perhaps you would be kind enough to draft a short review on the web site where you bought it?

Just a few words would be great.

It all helps.

Many thanks

Richard Harrison

30780998R00090

Printed in Great
Britain
by Amazon